Sensible Kate

Sensible Kate

A STORY BY DORIS GATES

Illustrated by Marjorie Torrey

▶P 76

New York

THE VIKING PRESS

1943

FIRST PUBLISHED SEPTEMBER 1943

Contents

Sensible Kate

Chapter I

The Question Mark in the Kitchen

KATE opened her eyes and sleepily watched the shadows moving on the ceiling over her head. They came from the walnut tree outside the window, thin lines that crossed each other, making tick-tack-toe, three-in-a-row patterns on the white wall paper. There were no leaves as yet, but the sun this morning was strong, though it was only February. Spring comes early in California, even at the seaside, and Kate knew it wouldn't be long before those thin lines sprouted other shadows and the tick-tack-toes would be spoiled.

She was thoroughly awake now but remained motionless under the bed quilts while her eyes, as round as an owl's and sharply critical, moved slowly over the room in a careful survey. What kind of housekeeping would be expected of her here? There had been no chance to find out last night as the shaded lamp on the dresser had left the corners of the room in shadow and Kate knew that corners were a dead giveaway. Turning her head now to peer into the one nearest the bed, she pulled into a straight line across the pillow the red braid which had lain crookedly there like a vein of rich ore in white granite. Relief and satisfaction lit for a moment her sober gray eyes. There wasn't one speck of dust nor the slightest suggestion of a cobweb. Mrs. Tuttle was evidently a better housekeeper than Cousin Ethel had been.

Kate's curiosity was more than merely idle. For an unknown length of time, she was to be a "family helper" in this household over which Mrs. Tuttle ruled. She knew from experience that there was apt to be less work in a neatly kept house than in a messy one. Her hopes for the future brightened and with them her interest in the two people with whom she had come to live.

Downstairs she could hear Mrs. Tuttle walking back and forth across the kitchen. She went in nervous, quick steps, quite different from Cousin Ethel's slippered shuffling. Should she get up now, or wait until she was called? Kate wondered. Perhaps the Tuttles would rather have breakfast by themselves. Since Mr. Tuttle had not come home until after she had gone to bed last night, it was possible that Mrs. Tuttle wanted to talk her over with him. It was hard not knowing what was expected of you and, for Kate, it was most un-usual.

Yesterday Miss Watson from the county office had brought her here to make her home with the Tuttles until further notice. Until a short time ago, she had lived with Cousin Ethel and her family. But their interest in her had proved so slight that when they decided to leave the state, they had turned Kate over to the county to be cared for as any other orphan would be. Kate couldn't even remember her father and mother, they had died such a long time ago. All she could remember was a bewildering succession of relatives who had taken a haphazard interest in her. But none of them had felt any real responsibility toward this red-headed and plain-faced little girl. Not even Cousin Ethel with whom she had lived the longest.

It was something of a relief, Kate thought, lying there and going back over yesterday's happenings, to know that some-one was now officially responsible for her. Even if that "some-one" was merely a bloodless thing called "the county." At least, it was someone and it might bring a little order and stability into her life. Kate liked order. It was the opposite of messiness and its presence gave you the feeling of knowing what you were about.

Looking at the whole thing another way, Kate could even feel an unaccustomed glow of importance at the thought of a whole county's making her its own particular responsibility. Counties were pretty important things. Pulling her knees up to make a hump in the bed's middle, Kate considered this angle of the matter, deciding at last that she wasn't so much *on* the county as *of* the county, one of its official family, so to speak. Like Miss Watson.

It was a good thought and went a long way toward restoring her confidence. Kate had liked Miss Watson. She had been kind and interested and had seemed to know how little girls felt about things.

"The Tuttles have no children, and they are very anxious to have you come and live with them," she had told Kate.

"You mean they want to adopt me?" Kate had demanded in alarm. It had always been a relief that none of her cousins had ever shown such a desire. It would be horrible to have to belong permanently to people whom you didn't care about. How did she know she'd like the Tuttles, or they her?

"No," Miss Watson had explained. "The county will pay them a certain sum every month for your board, but they will stand as parents to you."

"But won't I ever see you after I go to live with them?" Kate had asked.

"Most certainly you will," Miss Watson had reassured her. "I'll drop in every once in a while to make sure you're all getting along all right."

And so last evening they had driven to this little seaside town and to the Tuttles' front door. Mr. Tuttle who worked at the post office had not been home when they arrived. But Mrs. Tuttle was, of course, and had tried in a shy way to make Kate feel welcome. But Kate had not responded with much warmth. She had been passed around too many times to be impressed now. So she had slumped in her chair, her

14

freckled face giving no sign of what might be going on just back of her gray eyes. They were good eyes, grave and direct, but a little doubting on this occasion and after one or two unsuccessful efforts to erase that doubt, Mrs. Tuttle had ignored Kate, directing the whole of her nervous attention to Miss Watson.

"I'm sure you'll find Kate a very sensible child," Miss Watson had said on leaving.

It hadn't sounded very thrilling, then, and it didn't seem very thrilling now as Kate lay thinking about it. That was all anyone had ever been able to say in praise of her. She was sensible. Somehow it left a great deal to be desired. In the long catalogue of human endowments, it seemed a bitter thing that she should have drawn only good sense as her portion. Perhaps, she decided, it was all she had a right to expect. People with red hair and freckles couldn't expect very much. And it was undoubtedly better than nothing at all.

Like most people, Kate had definite ideas of what constituted feminine charm and beauty. Also she had sense, enough sense, in fact, to realize that in no slightest way did she fulfill her own standards of what charm and beauty consisted of. Her hair was straight and red, her features were nothing to speak of, and where her body should have curved gracefully, there were only sharp angles and hard muscles, like a boy's. In short, there wasn't the first thing cute about Kate and she knew it. And suffered accordingly. Because Kate longed above all things to be pretty and cute. If you were pretty, everyone was crazy about you, even your relatives. If you were cute, nothing was expected of you except cuteness. And if you were pretty and cute enough, you might even get into the movies.

Since these qualities which she so greatly valued were with all their glittering possibilities forever denied her, Kate had very sensibly cast about for a substitute, and, since being sensible didn't demand that you be cute, but only that you mind your p's and q's and do what is expected of you, Kate had taken good sense as her portion and had tried to make of it what she could. Still, down in her heart she knew, or thought she knew, that good sense wasn't really important. If you were only pretty enough or cute enough, it didn't matter in the least whether you had good sense or not. Anyway, that's what Kate thought and envied all little girls with curls.

It was quiet in the kitchen now. Probably Mr. and Mrs. Tuttle were eating their breakfast. The thought reminded Kate that she was hungry and she tossed back the covers and slid out of bed. For a moment she stood shivering in the middle of the little room while she tried to get the feel of having it entirely to herself. Always before, she had lived surrounded by cousins of assorted ages. It gave her a strange sense of dignity, almost of power, to know that this small domain tucked up under the gables of the old clapboard house was her own. She turned a possessive eye upon its white walls and ruffled window curtains. She could go over and shut that door and no one would try to stop her. It was the door to her room. Her very own. Kate at once crossed over and shut it. A splendid thrill of isolation and independence flooded her. Now Mr. and Mrs. Tuttle below stairs might as well have been somewhat long upper lip and his ears stood out from his head in a startled way. For an instant, they gazed silently at one another, the shy little girl and the shy little man. Then Mrs. Tuttle whirled from the stove, caught sight of Kate, and pounced upon her with bustling eagerness.

"Come right in, my dear," she said as Kate still stood uncertainly in the doorway. "I want to make you acquainted with Mr. Tuttle. This is the little girl who has come to live with us," turning to her husband. "I'm sure she's a very nice and sensible child and that we'll all be very happy together."

Kate wasn't at all sure, but felt no inclination to argue the matter. Time would doubtless take care of it, and there was nothing to worry about as long as they didn't want to adopt her. Just now, there was Mr. Tuttle to be reckoned with. Mrs. Tuttle seemed all right in an earnest, managing way. But what was her husband like? Kate looked at him again. A little pleading smile was beginning to show under the mousy mustache as he looked back at her, his head cocked a little to one side.

"I hope you'll like us," he said in a voice so low Kate could hardly hear him. But as the words did reach her and soaked down into her heart, she felt like reaching out to hug this funny little man who was evidently afraid of children. For all his shyness, for all his awkwardness, he had managed to think of just the right thing to say. It made Kate's own shyness vanish in a warm burst of friendliness, enabling her to say with certainty and sincerity, "I hope *you'll* like *me*."

The words just popping out of her like that without previous thought or planning so astonished Kate that she was completely tongue-tied immediately after they were spoken. She couldn't even answer Mr. Tuttle's quick smile before he ducked behind his newspaper again, but sat there worrying for fear she had said the wrong thing. She might have sat there indefinitely, as silent as a clam, if Mrs. Tuttle hadn't ended her embarrassment by asking, "Do you like your eggs turned over, or sunny-side up?"

Now Kate really preferred them turned over. But there was something in the words "sunny-side up" which exactly fitted the way she felt a second after the question was asked. It was a brand new feeling for Kate who had always just made the best of things and had always done what was expected of her. For the first time since she could remember, someone had actually cared how she felt about something. It was no wonder, then, that she should feel "sunny-side up." For the second time that morning, and within two minutes of the first, Kate acted on impulse.

"I'll have them sunny-side up, please," she said.

This time she was not so much astonished as pleased at her own unexpected behavior. Besides, the eggs were really good this way. Better even, she believed after sober consideration, than the other way.

Before Kate had finished her breakfast, Mr. Tuttle came out from behind the newspaper and jerked his watch out of his pocket. He glanced hastily at it, muttered, "Gracious, I must be going," and shoved back his chair.

Had Kate possessed a better knowledge of nonsense than she did, she might have thought that Mr. Tuttle very much resembled a certain famous white rabbit, whiskers and all. And she might have half-expected him to say, "Oh dear, oh dear, I shall be too late," and dart into a hole in the wall. But knowing nothing about *Alice in Wonderland,* she missed the fun of all this and merely watched curiously as Mr. Tuttle gave Mrs. Tuttle a peck on the cheek, nodded at Kate, and hurried out of the kitchen, the newspaper making a meek little crackling as he crushed it into his coat pocket.

"Mr. Tuttle isn't long on talk," his wife explained to Kate while she poured herself another cup of coffee. "But it's just his way. He's naturally quiet and doesn't mean to be grouchy or anything like that. I don't believe I ever saw him really angry."

She stopped the cup half-way to her lips as she searched back over the years for a forgotten glimpse of Mr. Tuttle in a towering rage. Then she shook her head. "No, I can't remember when I've ever seen him downright mad."

"I like him," said Kate.

"Everybody likes him," said Mrs. Tuttle matter-of-factly. "He's as good a man as ever lived and a fine provider. I've known every day of my married life right where my next meal was coming from. I tell you not every woman can say that."

Kate munched a piece of toast and thought this over carefully. Mrs. Tuttle's married life had differed considerably from life as she had been living it up to yesterday. There hadn't been a good provider in her whole cousinage, she decided. There had been food, of course, but often the meals were sketchy and irregular. It was astonishing that this mild little man could accomplish what her husky relatives had consistently failed to do. It was certainly going to be different living here. No more shiftless, easy-going, disorderly days. Already, Kate could feel a clocklike precision in the Tuttle household. Being an orderly, cut-and-dried sort of person herself, she responded happily to the new atmosphere. It made sense, and it gave her a feeling of security, a thing which she had experienced only in small measure up to now. This kind of living might be less exciting than the old, but there was much to be said for it just the same. And she felt sure that Mrs. Tuttle's brisk managing would be a lot easier to endure than Cousin Ethel's whining uselessness.

After the dishes were dried and put away, Mrs. Tuttle explained to Kate what the rest of the morning routine would consist of. Tomorrow she would be going to school, but today she would have all to herself when the necessary duties of a well-ordered household had been performed. First of all, she must make her bed. Then she must tidy up her room. On Saturdays she would, of course, help with the cleaning. But on school mornings, doing the dishes and putting her room in order would complete her duties until late afternoon when she would be expected to help with the dinner and with the dishes afterward.

Mrs. Tuttle explained everything in a very definite way, as if she thought Kate might object and argue about it. But Kate thought her tasks not only simple but extremely light. Cousin Ethel had demanded lots more of her, and in every cousin's house in which she had lived, there had been a baby or two. Babies made an endless amount of work. But thinking back over those days now as she plumped the pillow and

22

laid it neatly against the headboard of her little white bed, Kate realized that the babies had been the nicest part of it all. She was going to feel the lack of babies in the Tuttle house.

"Wouldn't you like to look around a bit?" Mrs. Tuttle asked when Kate came downstairs. "I always think it helps to settle you down if you get the lay of the land first thing. Our street will take you right down to the ocean if you follow it long enough."

Without waiting for Mrs. Tuttle to change her mind or to find some last minute thing for her to do, in case she happened to be that kind of person, Kate immediately put on her coat and went outside.

Chapter II

Edge of Land

NEXT door to the Tuttle house stood a dark old dwelling, its front windows completely shaded by an ancient cypress. Kate stood on the sidewalk in front of it and gazed up at its second-story windows. The blinds had been closely drawn, giving an air of mystery to the place. Around the cypress, a violet bed spread its deep color over the moist earth, and standing there, Kate caught the fresh scent of hundreds of tiny flowers.

There is something about the scent of violets. It is more than irresistible. It is compelling. Forgetting for the moment that she had absolutely no business in any front yard except the Tuttles', Kate all at once felt her feet moving one after the other up the mossy brick walk toward the dark old house and the violet bed. There her feet stopped while Kate took a careful look around. The windows of the old house seemed to accuse her with blind eyes. But there was no one actually there to see.

So Kate squatted on her heels and reached toward the flowers. Eagerly she slid her fingers down the stem of one of them. But before she could pluck it free, she jerked her hand away and stuck a hurting finger in her mouth. Something

24

had pricked her. Something like tiny sharp teeth had buried itself there and now as she drew it out of her mouth to look at it, she could see little beads of blood slowly forming on it.

Kate leaned closer to inspect the plants. To say the least, it was most peculiar because violets do not sting people. Warily, she parted the green leaves. Now she could see what had caused the trouble. Growing close to the roots of the flowers and intermingled freely with them, were little round knobs of gray-green cactus, their sloping sides bristling with myriads of stiff little thorns. It would be practically impossible, she discovered, to pick the violets without coming into contact with the cactus.

Kate rose slowly to her feet and stared at the old house. Had someone witnessed her discomfort? Was someone craftily edging back a blind to gloat secretly over this trespasser? The thought was maddening to Kate who prided herself on minding her p's and q's. She felt her face begin to glow with tell-tale warmth. But the windows remained as closely shaded as before, not a blind twitched anywhere. Only, at Kate's feet, the scent of violets rose mockingly.

Even a duller brain than Kate's, which was by no means dull, could easily have guessed that not by accident were cactus and violets sharing the same bed. They were put there and for a reason. She sensed that reason almost at once and with that sensing, resentment rose so swiftly in her that it quite wiped out all the humiliation she had been feeling.

"Whoever lives here, doesn't care for children," she said out loud, hoping that someone would hear her. "Whoever lives here is mean, downright mean. Only someone who hates

25

children would be mean enough to plant cactus in a violet bed. And I'll bet the violets hate it too!"

That last was just thrown in because Kate couldn't think of anything better to say. She knew perfectly well that violets have no power to hate anything, being merely flowers, but now she was too angry to bother to talk sensibly.

Unhappily for Kate's frame of mind, the old house continued blind and indifferent to her outburst. So, feeling baffled in addition to everything else, she turned at last and walked back over the mossy bricks to the street with what dignity she could muster and continued her stroll oceanward.

Her anger diminished, though, as she walked along. So did the pain in her finger. In fact, the two disappeared together almost as if they had been one and the same thing. Kate's temper was quick and as flaming as her hair, but she had too much good sense to brood long over something she could do nothing about. Besides, she rebuked herself, if she had minded her p's and q's like a really sensible person, she would never have got mixed up with the cactus in the first place. Unhappily, the business of being sensible is not always simple, as Kate had already found out.

The street was unpaved and tree-lined with most of its houses set in heavily wooded gardens. It was almost like walking out in the country. The air was sweet with the smell of wet earth, salt water, and wood smoke from hidden chimneys. Good smells, all of them, Kate thought, her freckled nose sniffing them hungrily. Unconsciously, she began to walk faster as the salt smell grew stronger. At last, topping a little rise, she saw where the road ended in a wall of blue, and

26

flinging decorum to the wind that carried her pigtails out behind her, Kate began to run.

In another moment, she was standing on a high bluff at the very edge of land. Out in front of her stretched endless limits of blue water and far below her the white surf lapped and curled. As if they had never been, Kate forgot cactus, violets, and even the unknown person who didn't like children in the thrill of knowing that at this very moment there was nothing between her own small self and China but this particular body of water with perhaps a few islands in between. This spot on which she stood was the jumping-off place on every map. It was a wonderful thought and made her feel the way closing the door to her room had made her feel.

The sunlight glinting on the moving surface of the water seemed to Kate brighter than anything had ever been before, and the wind blowing into her face bore the scent of a thousand tides. Here was the world suddenly fresh and clear and radiant.

Kate felt radiant, too. Every inch of her tingled and a strange excitement flowed with the blood in her veins. It was all so big and sparkly! Why she'd bet even Cousin Ethel would feel alive if she could stand where she, Kate, was standing now.

No one could be drab and listless in the presence of this. Wouldn't it be a fine thing, she thought, if all the Cousin Ethels in the world could be brought here to the edge of land? A fine thing for them and a fine thing for the world. But what would you call them after they woke up and stopped their whining? Because, of course, all this would wake them up and make their whining seem ridiculous They wouldn't be Cousin Ethels any more. At this idea, Kate laughed foolishly for about the first time in her life and so startled a wheeling gull that he cried aloud and slid sideways on the wind away from her.

Kate might have gone on for the rest of the morning thinking mixed-up thoughts about Cousin Ethel, China, and blue water if a voice behind her hadn't suddenly recalled her to the fact that she wasn't teetering on the edge of a map, after all, but standing sturdily at the very end of a village street.

"Hello, there," said the voice, and Kate turned to face a young man who was smiling pleasantly around a pipe stem gripped in one corner of his mouth. His hair was almost as red as Kate's, and his eyes were exactly the color of the water out beyond them, and almost as sparkly.

"Hello," returned Kate, grave again as she studied the newcomer and waited for him to say something else. If there was to be any conversation, he would have to start it, since she had arrived here first and had been getting along very happily until he came. Whether she stayed or not would now depend entirely upon his next remark. She was hardly prepared for it when it came.

"Don't move," suddenly commanded the strange young man. "Stand right where you are." He snatched the pipe from his mouth and, squinting up his eyes, stared hard at Kate.

She was too astonished to do anything but obey. She was a little frightened, too. It makes you a bit uneasy when standing not over twelve inches from a straight drop into the Pacific Ocean to hear someone tell you not to move. Had the soles of Kate's feet sent down tendrils into the cliff, she couldn't have stood more firmly rooted.

"I never thought I'd live to see the day," said the man amazedly. "Red hair, pigtails, and all."

Kate knew he wasn't talking to her, so she kept silent until this fit or whatever had occasioned his strange conduct should pass off.

At last the man put the pipe back into his mouth, unsquinted his eyes, and smiling once more said to Kate, "Well, who are you and what have you got to say for yourself?"

"My name is Kate Summers," she replied, "and the only thing that can be said for me is that I am sensible."

Once more the stranger removed the pipe from his mouth and stared at Kate. Only this time his eyes were wide and unbelieving.

"What did you say?" he demanded like one who thinks he hasn't heard correctly.

"I said my name is Kate Summers and that I am sensible and that's all."

"I'm Christopher Cline, Kate," said the man, advancing now and offering his hand to the little girl, "and I haven't got a lick of sense. And neither has Nora. You should be good for us."

"Who's Nora?" asked Kate, shaking Christopher's hand.

"She's my wife and the bravest woman in the world."

"Is she?" asked Kate, interested at once. "What did she do to be so brave?"

29

"She married me," said Christopher, and Kate felt terribly let down. People got married every day. She couldn't see how it would take any special courage to marry this man. He looked friendly and harmless.

"Where do you live?" asked Christopher.

"Down the street," Kate wagged her head toward the direction from which she had come, "with the Tuttles. I'm an orphan and the county pays them for my board."

Might as well get it over and settled. He probably knew, anyway, that the Tuttles had no children and would only wonder how it happened that they had one now.

Christopher nodded his head understandingly and looked at Kate without a trace of pity. "They are fine people, the Tuttles," he said. "You're lucky."

"I have my own room, too," Kate added.

"Very lucky," said Christopher, pulling furiously on his pipe which began to send long blue clouds out over the ocean.

A silence fell between them. Not an awkward silence, but an easy kind, the sort that comes in a conversation when one person is going over in his mind what the other person has said. The kind of silence that can only come between people who are good listeners as well as good talkers. Both Kate and Christopher were gazing out to sea.

" 'Silent upon a peak in Darien,' " said Christopher.

"What?" asked Kate.

"It's part of a poem," explained Christopher, "and I just happened to think of it."

"Are you a poet?" Kate asked, her voice a little fearful.

She had always believed poets to be highly impractical people. All the accounts she had ever read of them in school pictured them as starving to death. Christopher looked well fed, however.

"No," replied Christopher. "I'm something much worse. I'm an artist."

"Oh," said Kate. Artists were also, she believed, highly impractical people.

"That's what everyone says when they discover the awful truth." Christopher sighed. "Everyone except Nora. And yet I'm really a harmless fellow. Why should it be a crime to paint pictures, Kate?"

He turned toward her as if he really wanted to know. So Kate considered his question carefully before answering. She knew that Cousin Ethel and her husband had held artists in great scorn because when Roger, who was their son, had shown definite abilities in that direction, they had sent a note to school demanding that such time wasting must be stopped as they intended Roger to be a mechanic, or something equally useful and successful in life. It was a pity, Kate thought, as she considered this attractive and friendly person, that he should be unsuccessful. Perhaps it was not too late yet for him to become a mechanic if only he would put his mind on it. It never occurred to her that Christopher might not be a successful mechanic.

"I didn't know it was a crime to want to paint pictures," she said slowly, "but it isn't a very good way to make a living. I suppose that's what's bothering you, because that's mainly the thing that bothers everybody. I've noticed that the

33

people who are making a living at something usually feel all right about it."

Christopher looked at her again as if he hadn't heard correctly.

"How old are you, Kate?"

"I'm ten."

"You've done quite a bit of living in your ten years, haven't you?"

Kate didn't answer, and Christopher studied her over the top of his pipe. At last he smiled and there was something in his smile that almost made Kate smile back, but not quite. Kate didn't smile easily.

"What gives you the notion that you have good sense?" he asked at last. "It isn't often we recognize it in ourselves."

For a moment Kate hesitated, then she remembered the smile and decided to talk. "Well, you see," she began, "whenever anyone wants to say anything nice about me, they can't think of anything except that I'm sensible so they always say I'm a sensible child. I'm not cute and I'm not pretty. I'm just sensible."

" 'Just sensible,' " repeated the man, quietly. "I should think that that might be at least as rewarding as being cute. And in the long run it might wear better than being pretty."

"Perhaps," replied Kate dubiously. "The only trouble is that nobody knows you're sensible just by looking at you, and when you're homely like me, they may not take the trouble to get acquainted with you to find out."

Christopher pondered this somewhat mixed-up speech for

several seconds before he said, "I guess I'm different then. When it comes to little girls, I think I prefer them homely. When they're cute, they haven't time for anything but the business of being cute and it bores me. And when they're pretty, they're too apt to know about it and too anxious about wanting everyone else to know it, too."

"You seem to know quite a lot about little girls," observed Kate, something close to awe in her voice.

"As an artist, it's my business to be observant," replied the man.

Kate was impressed. There might be something to be said for artists, after all. But he hadn't convinced her. Slowly she shook her head.

"Just the same," she declared stoutly, "I'd rather be pretty than sensible."

"Why?" asked Christopher.

"Because if you're just sensible, you always have to do what's expected of you, and if you're pretty, people don't seem to care. I get very tired of always doing what's expected of me."

Christopher laughed. "Why not change the pattern and do the unexpected some day, just for fun?"

Kate thought a moment, eyes squinted against the light from the sea. She was thinking of a violet bed and cactus and a hurt finger. Again she shook her head.

"No," she said, "I'd better stick to being just sensible. After all, a person has to have something, and I'd better make the most of what I've got. Being sensible is better than not being anything at all."

"You know, Kate," said Christopher, breaking the silence her words had brought between them. "You know, you've learned a lot of wisdom in your ten years. I shouldn't be at all surprised if by the end of another ten, you might not be wise as well as sensible. And very often wise people are beautiful."

"Why?" asked Kate, a sudden throbbing in her throat.

"Because," answered the man, "wisdom is beautiful and when people possess it, they seem to possess its beauty at the same time. It sort of looks out of their faces."

Kate moved a little closer to Christopher, so close that she could reach out her hand and lay it on his arm. She needed something to steady herself against, for her knees felt suddenly weak and her heart was beating fast enough to choke her. Here was someone saying as if he really knew, that you *might* someday become beautiful just by becoming wise, and somehow wisdom was mixed up with being sensible!

"How do you get to be wise?" she asked almost in a whisper.

And like the kind fairy in an old tale, her new friend gave her the answer.

"By keeping your eyes and mind and heart open," he said.

Kate's face was suddenly alight and almost lovely in its shining eagerness. "Oh, I will, I *will*," she cried.

"It's a promise, then," said Christopher.

He put out his hand and Kate laid hers in it. For a moment they looked into each other's eyes and Kate found herself smiling without any trouble at all.

"Bless you," said Christopher heartily. "And now won't you come over to our house? I want Nora to meet you. She could do with a dash of sensible Kate, and I think you could do with a little nonsense, my dear."

Chapter III

Lighthouse Avenue

THEY walked back to the Tuttles' together. Kate thought
she shouldn't go visiting without Mrs. Tuttle's consent,
and Christopher agreed with her. It was fun to be walking
beside Christopher; good to feel his friendliness. As they approached the dark old house where she had suffered her humiliation, Kate surveyed it without a trace of bitterness. How
different was her return home from her going forth!

Now she had a friend, an artist who knew about becoming
wise and maybe beautiful. She could even feel a little sorry
for the unknown person who didn't like children! Such a person would have no friends surely. But she had Christopher,
and she was reasonably certain that if he had a garden there
would be no cactus in it. Or, if there were, it would not be
mixed with the violets. Everything would be in its proper
place, neat and tidy. Because Kate recognized in Christopher
the kind of person who was thoroughly likable and it would
have been impossible for her to like anyone who was messy.
Without the shadow of a doubt, Christopher and very likely
Nora, too, for wasn't she his own wife, were as neat as Mrs.
Tuttle. With more eagerness than she usually felt about
things, Kate looked forward to her visit with the Clines.

Mrs. Tuttle was entirely willing that she should go. "But don't stay for lunch," she warned Kate. "You don't want to wear out your welcome right at the start."

"No danger," said Christopher, politely.

Kate promised not to stay too long and the two started off.

"We live on Lighthouse Avenue, one block over," said Christopher as they came to the corner.

"Is there a lighthouse on it?" Kate asked eagerly.

"No, and I guess there never has been. I think it was named that to give the tourist population a little local color. But Nora says it's because nobody on it does any other kind of house-keeping."

This sounded a little Cousin Ethelish to Kate and therefore somewhat alarming. But she quieted her fears. Probably Nora had been making a joke when she said it. Kate had always had a little difficulty in recognizing a joke. For her, they just didn't make sense. Now, however, she couldn't help hoping that Nora had been joking.

But misgivings settled heavily upon Kate when after about five minutes of walking Christopher said, "Here it is," and stopped before a small dwelling which looked as if it were holding itself upright only long enough to decide which way to fall. Even the picket fence around the tangle of garden was rickety, its gate letting forth a cry of agony when Christopher opened it for Kate to pass through. For a moment, she hesi- tated. There was a familiarity about all this that made her feel a sudden wild urge to race back to the Tuttles where all was order and precision. For this run-down little house with its uncared-for garden could easily have been the dwelling

39

place of any one of her cousins, and Kate was reasonably certain that she wanted no part of it.

And it was the home of Christopher, of all people! Christopher whom she liked more already than she had ever liked any other person! Christopher living in a messy-looking ramshackle house! It was disappointing and upsetting. Very upsetting, because, strangely enough, she still liked him. About as much as ever.

She looked again at the house, hoping to find some redeeming feature about it, and then she made an interesting discovery. Somehow the little house didn't look drab or forlorn as those of her cousins had. It wore its sun-curled shingles and its peeling paint with a jaunty air like a small boy who defiantly sports a badly battered and dearly beloved straw hat. Perhaps that was because Christopher lived there. No house could seem forlorn with Christopher in it. So, feeling a little comforted, Kate passed through the gate and walked hopefully up the path to the front door.

Kate should have been warned as to Nora, for Christopher had told her right at the beginning that neither one of them had a lick of sense. But she hadn't remembered, and anyway it would have been an insufficient warning for what met her eyes on entering the Cline living-room. The first thing she saw, because it was right smack in the middle of the room, was an easel supporting a half-finished portrait of a man, which, because of its red hair, Kate supposed to be Christopher. Except for this detail, however, it bore not the least resemblance to him. Before the easel sat a young woman in a paint-smeared smock. Her hair was in the wildest disorder and her pretty face was daubed here and there with streaks of mixed color and other streaks which Kate easily recognized as tears.

"Oh, Chris," she wailed as they came into the room, "it just won't go the way it should. It's no good and neither am I. Whatever gave me the idea I could paint?"

With that Nora buried her face in her hands and burst into noisy sobs. Now, suddenly, Kate remembered what Christopher had said and heartily agreed with him. Nora obviously didn't have a lick of sense. She felt not the slightest sympathy for her tears and wondered how Christopher could as she watched him cross the room and put an arm around his wife.

It was ridiculous for a grown-up to cry. Besides, it made you feel as if you had no business being around. To cover her confusion and embarrassment, Kate averted her eyes from Nora's too open misery to survey critically and with mounting disapproval this room into which she had been ushered and in the next moment abandoned. Having seen Nora, Kate was in no way surprised. It looked just as she would have expected it to look. Plainly, Nora was no better housekeeper than was Cousin Ethel.

The little stone fireplace in the corner was half-choked with ashes. Their pale dust lay along the mantel in a smooth coating of gray. That shelf hadn't been dusted in well over a week, Kate surmised expertly. Not for nothing was she a family helper! On the mantel, in happy confusion, was a can opener, a bunch of keys, and some tubes of paint all mixed up with books and vases and some candlesticks. Only to Kate, it didn't seem a happy mixture. Unaccustomed though she might be to such elegant interior adornments as candlesticks, her common sense told her that can openers could have no rightful place beside them. Clearly, Nora was shiftless, and Christopher, who was a really nice person, was to be pitied.

At about the same moment that Kate reached this conclusion, Nora drew away from Christopher to notice her small visitor for the first time. It was really Christopher who shifted her attention. Exactly, Kate thought, like someone dangling a toy before a crying baby, he said, "Look, dear, I've brought someone to see you. This is Kate."

"Hello," said Nora. "Did you ever see such a mess?"

"No," replied Kate honestly, "I never did."

Evidently Nora was unprepared for such perfect agreement. Perhaps she had even assumed that Kate would politely deny the existence of a mess at all. If so, she didn't know Kate. For a moment she simply stared at her young caller exactly as Christopher had stared out on the cliff. Only Nora's brown eyes were twinkling, and the corners of her mouth twitched. Then, in the next moment she was laughing, laughing with as gay abandon as a short time before she had wept bitterly. Christopher was chuckling and Kate wondered what had got into them. She could see nothing to laugh at. She had merely given a straight answer to a straight question, and there was certainly nothing funny about that. Grown-ups could be very puzzling at times, and very irritating, too.

At length Nora stopped laughing and stretched out a hand to Kate. "You're priceless," she said, "and I'm really glad you've come. Forgive my bad behavior a moment ago. I was feeling wretched, but now everything is all right again. Christopher always knows what's good for me. Yesterday, it was a stray kitten. This morning, it's you."

Now when Nora stretched out a hand to Kate and began talking in such a friendly way, Kate had been almost willing to forgive her, for Christopher's sake, at least. But as she went on talking, Kate's charity gave way to a feeling of deep indignation. It was far from flattering to have herself lumped with a stray kitten as something good for Nora. It made Kate feel as if she were still being dangled on a string in front of Nora's pert nose.

The picture it presented seemed a most undignified one and the longer she contemplated it in her mind's eye, the less it appealed to her. Deciding to resent it as unbecoming to someone who had come in all good faith to this house only to be received as a stray kitten might be received, Kate drew herself up and said with all the dignity that ten years of living had bestowed upon her, "I'm glad I met you, and now I must go home."

In the sudden silence which followed her remark, Kate got almost to the door. But before she could quite reach it, she found her way barred by a very earnest and red-headed young man who placed a hand on each of her shoulders and, looking deep into her angry eyes, said,

"Don't go, please. You've only just got here and Nora meant no unkindness. Besides, she needs you. Really she does."

Kate looked over her shoulder at Nora who still sat perched

43

in front of the big easel, her paint-stained hands folded quietly in her lap. All laughter had gone out of her and her body drooped listlessly. She looked very lonely and very young sitting there and when she raised her eyes to Kate's and said, "The kitten stayed almost an hour before it left me," Kate all at once made up her mind about Nora.

Being needed by someone is quite different from being merely good for someone. Kate could sense the difference in the way Nora had spoken and in the way she looked. She was lonely and discouraged and, for some strange reason, both she and Christopher believed that a little girl with red hair and good sense was what she needed.

Kate's indignation vanished, leaving in its place pride and satisfaction. Not many times in her life had anyone needed her. And then not for her good sense. Always she had been the one who had done the needing. Of course she had only needed simple things like food and clothing and shelter. Nora needed none of these. She needed comfort, the comfort of a plaything, and somehow, Kate knew, she would have to provide it. It was expected of her.

"I'll stay," she announced calmly and, being ten years old, was pleasantly gratified at the effect of her words.

Nora's head came up, her brown eyes dancing once more, while Christopher let out a long whistle of relief.

"That was a near one, Kate," he said. "For a moment there, I thought you were a goner."

Kate scowled self-consciously as she pulled off her coat.

"I'll be one, too, if you don't let me clean up this room. It's

44

worse than Cousin Ethel's and I couldn't bear to sit in it for even a minute."

There was nothing so good for a case of the blues as a dose of housework, Kate remembered. A little stirring around would shake Nora out of herself.

But that young woman set up a good-natured howl. "Spare my blushes," she begged, "and spare the dust. I'm an artist, not a housekeeper."

Kate glanced at the terrible portrait of Christopher.

"No, I'm going to clean, and you'll have to help me," she said firmly. "I couldn't get through in time and Mrs. Tuttle told me not to stay for lunch."

If Nora couldn't paint any better than that, it was high time she learned to keep house, Kate thought.

"A bossy brat, isn't she?" Nora grinned up at her husband.

"Rather, my dear, rather," he replied with mock seriousness, "but not without justification. Woman's place, you know."

Nora made a face at him then turned toward the picture. For a moment she sat studying it disgustedly. At last, slowly, she rose from her chair.

"Kate," she said, "don't ever aim higher than your talents. It'll only cause you misery."

"I won't," promised Kate cheerfully as she considered which part of the room they should begin on first, and with not the slightest idea of what Nora was talking about.

Together, they began to clean the room while Christopher, with the best intentions in the world, was mostly in the way.

45

Finally, they chased him out altogether and he disappeared town-ward, whistling happily.

Happily, too, Kate and Nora put the tiny house in order. It was fun, Kate thought, to tackle a house as messy as this one. You could really see where you left off and, when a room was finally in perfect order, you had a sense of real achievement. There would be little satisfaction in cleaning Mrs. Tuttle's living-room. It would be just a case of going through the proper motions. No part of it would look better after a thorough sweeping and dusting than it had looked before, because Mrs. Tuttle was an immaculate house-keeper.

Nora, however, was entirely different. Kate knew very well as she dug into corners and set furniture to rights that there would be many opportunities at the Clines's to satisfy any urge she might feel for a real work-out. And it would be a grand excuse for coming back again. After one hour with Nora, Kate knew she wanted to come back. Of course, Nora didn't have a lick of sense, but her nonsense was so delightful that several times Kate caught herself giggling.

There was the instance when she had gone up to the gas range with a wet scrub rag in her hand, "And now I'll wash your little face," she had said, wiping the oven door briskly. Of course, it was silly, but Kate had to smile even now, a half hour later, at the idea of a gas range having a little face.

In fact, when Nora had caught Kate's look of amazement that any grown-up should act in this way, she had defended herself by insisting that all objects had personalities of their own and that a very great writer had made himself famous

46

Torrey

with stories about them. Whereupon, she had told Kate of Hans Christian Andersen, and suddenly, to Kate's utter astonishment, there they both were, sitting in the midst of the mess while Nora told his story of the darning needle and Kate sat entranced, forgetting entirely that she had thought she couldn't sit down in such a rumpled room.

After that, Kate was never to look upon anything with quite the same eyes she had used before. Something had been added, an inner eye which saw things differently, but which saw them just as clearly and perhaps more truly. Was this what Christopher had meant when he said she needed nonsense? Whatever it was, Kate was thankful to have discovered it.

Cleaning house proved a fine way of getting acquainted, too. Perhaps the story helped. Anyway, before they were finished, Nora had learned the more important facts of Kate's brief existence. And Kate, in turn, had found out that Nora and Christopher were in high disfavor with their respective families because Nora's husband insisted upon being an artist instead of working sensibly in his father's office.

"He'd make more money doing that, wouldn't he?" asked Kate carefully dusting a lopsided vase and wondering why Nora kept such a thing around when you could get any number of really good ones at the five-and-ten.

"Oh, probably he could," said Nora, "but there're lots more important things in life than making money."

"What, for instance?" Kate could remember some of Cousin Ethel's opinions on this subject and only this morning Mrs. Tuttle had praised her own husband's abilities as a provider. Together, they had definitely colored her own thinking. Nora just didn't have good sense.

"Well, being happy, for one, and having the courage of your own convictions, for another; and being independent."

On the last word, Nora set her mouth defiantly giving a vicious rub on the cupboard door she was scrubbing. Kate thought she looked a million miles away from the Nora she had seen sitting in front of the easel. And, somehow, an apron seemed to become her better than a smock. She looked neater in it and more business-like. But, of course, she didn't have good sense, as her remark just now clearly proved. However, Kate being a little girl didn't say so, but held her tongue respectfully, and went right on liking Nora better than ever.

At last the little house was clean and shining. Everything was in its proper place and would stay there, Nora affirmed, for perhaps three minutes after Christopher got home.

"Then he'll hang his coat over that chair," she said, pointing, "and he'll fill his pipe and spill tobacco there," pointing again, "and then he'll suddenly realize that we have moved his painting things and in a panic he'll get them all out and spread them over the whole room. After that, he'll settle down very happily in the mess and feel right with the world."

"But the dust will be gone," said Kate.

Nora laughed. "Yes, my child, the dust will be gone and my sacred pride will remain intact. Come. Let's take a look at the garden before you go."

As they emerged into the sunlight, Kate noticed a strange sweetness in the air which hadn't been there earlier in the day. It was as if the sun, gathering strength as it climbed the steep slope of the sky, had drawn the perfume from some secret place.

"Smell it," commanded Nora. "Was ever anything sweeter in February than China lilies?"

Kate didn't bother to sniff on purpose as Nora was doing since she had been smelling them all along. Instead, she looked carefully around, but could see no China lilies anywhere. It was no wonder, she thought, with such a tangle of weeds and shrubs covering the ground.

"I don't see them," she said, her tone heavy with disapproval.

Nora whirled toward her delightedly. "Of course you don't," she cried. "That's what's so charming about our garden. It's like a little wilderness hiding secrets from us. It won't offer up its good things unless we look for them. The China lilies are on the other side of that privet hedge. Come on, I'll show you."

She went at a trot through the bright green grass from which the dew had not yet quite evaporated. Kate followed dubiously, well aware that her shoes were getting wet and wondering if Mrs. Tuttle would mind. Any grown-up other than Nora would have more sense than to go running around a garden in this way. Sometimes Nora was provokingly unlike a grown-up at all, and as much trouble as Cousin Ethel's youngest. And just as easy to love. Yes, Kate had to admit, Nora was Nora and she wouldn't have changed her for the world.

Then she saw the China lilies. Not just a thin row of them or a few scattered clumps. They filled one whole corner of the garden with yellow and cream and green. They must have been growing here for years and years to have spread themselves like that. They were beautiful and the grass, unkemptly edging them round, contrasted pleasantly with their own stiff and upright green.

"Isn't it marvelous that no one has disturbed them?" said Nora. "The whole garden is like that. Every day it shares a secret with us. Sometimes Christopher gets the secret first, and sometimes I do. And whoever is given it, makes the other fellow guess. Secrets are lots of fun. Don't you think so, Kate?"

Kate didn't answer. She was thinking of what Nora had said about a garden giving you secrets. And she was thinking about how beautiful the China lilies were because no one had tried to make them neat. And she was remembering how sweet the lilies had smelled when she and Nora stood on the doorstep, and yet no one could have guessed where they grew unless he shared the secret of their whereabouts. And all at once, standing there in the sunlight close to Nora, Kate knew she wouldn't want this changed any more than she wanted Nora changed.

It was right just as it was. It was Nora's and Christopher's garden. It was Nora and Christopher. It was Lighthouse Avenue. She liked it, even though it was messy. Even though she didn't quite understand why she liked it.

"Don't you think secrets are fun, Kate?" Nora repeated.

"I never had a secret with anyone," said Kate, not sorrowfully, but merely stating a fact. "The people I've been with never bothered with such things." Cousin Ethel's family passed in review before her mind's eye and she added, "They just weren't secret people, I guess."

For a moment, Nora just stood quietly not saying anything. Then she reached out and turned Kate around so that she was facing her. Then she did a strange thing. She took Kate's face in her two hands. Kate instinctively drew back, but Nora held her firmly and she had to stand still. Kate's eyes were uneasy, though. What was Nora going to do? She felt helpless in the grasp of those cool, slender hands. And she also felt a little silly. Nora was certainly a most unexpected person. What was worse, you never knew what was expected of you around her. It was most upsetting.

"Do you know," said Nora, still holding Kate's face in her two hands, "I think you are a secret person. You are also an understanding person with good sense. I am going to tell you a secret."

She dropped her hands and watched Kate until the uneasy look had faded out of her eyes and one of surprise and expectancy had taken its place. This would be her first secret, and by the way Nora was acting, it must be a very important one. It was wonderful to be trusted like this! Again Kate felt as she had felt at the edge of land, sort of high up and unapproachable.

She looked straight back at Nora and said with great certainty and no little pride, "I'll keep the secret. I won't tell anyone at all. I promise."

With that, Nora leaned forward and whispered something into Kate's ear. Kate gasped, and every bit of soberness left her face.

"Oh, really, Nora? *Really?*" she cried.

Nora put a finger on her lips. "Sh-h-h. It's a secret. Remember."

"Oh, I'll remember, Nora. Every time you see me, you can know that I'll be remembering. And we won't tell anybody. Not even Christopher."

"Not even Christopher?" asked Nora. "Suppose he should guess?"

"Well, if he guesses, of course we can't help it," said Kate, her face serious again. "Only if he does, don't tell me, and don't let him tell me. I'd rather think it was just between you and me. It will seem more like our very own secret then."

"It's a bargain," said Nora. "And now," glancing at her wrist, "it's really lunch time. You'd better run along home since you said Mrs. Tuttle was expecting you. We can have hamburgers together another time. We have them often."

So Kate said good-by to Nora and walked through the squeaky little gate, shutting it carefully behind her. It was nice to be going back to Mrs. Tuttle's neat kitchen for lunch. It was good to know she was expected. She was glad she lived there. But oh, it was good, too, to know that Lighthouse Avenue, with all it held and all it promised, was only three blocks away!

Chapter IV

Valentines and Beverly Jean

THE next day, which was St. Valentine's, saw Kate on her way to school. No one went with her. Mrs. Tuttle had wanted to go, but Kate had begged to go alone. New schools held no terrors for her, and she knew that Mrs. Tuttle's inexperience at this sort of thing would only attract the wrong kind of attention to them. Everyone in town knew that Mrs. Tuttle had no children and to appear with her, therefore, would cause more curiosity about her background than Kate considered necessary or desirable right at first.

It was all very well to be proud of having a county responsible for you. It might be another thing to make others feel your pride. To them, you might still seem to be "on" the county. Cousin Ethel, for all her lack of interest, had been a cousin and therefore some family to lean on. It would probably be difficult to make others understand that being "of" the county had a special importance about it. Much better to let them assume she was just like any other child, until they learned differently. They would learn soon enough. So Kate went to school alone.

Without difficulty, she found the principal's office and in very short order, she was standing in the fifth grade room. It was almost nine o'clock and the children were already coming in, so Miss Morgan, the teacher, had little time to give Kate.

"Just sit there for the present," she said to her, indicating a desk near her own. "I'll attend to you when everyone is settled."

It had a disciplinary sound but Kate was not worried. She had been disposed of in this way before. With mild interest, she watched the boys and girls come into the room, go to their seats, and fix their frankly curious stares upon her. They were like children anywhere, she noted with satisfaction, and wondered which among them would be her special friend. By the time the bell rang, every seat in the room was occupied except the one across the aisle from Kate.

"Does anyone know what has happened to Beverly Jean this morning?" Miss Morgan asked.

"Oh, she'll be here," said a girl sitting near Kate and there followed a rambling recital of the reason for Beverly Jean's tardiness.

Miss Morgan's interest in the excuse did not seem to be very great, because long before the girl had finished with it, Miss Morgan was busy with somebody else. It was almost, thought Kate, as if she had heard the same thing many times before and didn't have to listen. Evidently Beverly Jean was often late.

Then someone entered the room. She didn't simply walk in. She entered. "There's Beverly Jean," cried several little girls all at once, and now, with the attention of the whole room focused on her, Beverly Jean moved down the aisle.

Kate watched her come with mingled feelings of unbelief and amazement. It couldn't be possible. It just couldn't happen. But, miraculously, it undoubtedly had. Here was Kate's dream come true. Here was everything she wanted to be and never could be.

To look at this girl, thought Kate, was the same as standing in front of a mirror and seeing reflected there the thing you wanted to see. Had she been suddenly granted the power to assemble just those details of physical perfection she most wanted herself, she couldn't have done a better job than this. It was exactly as if the word "cute" had been given a face and form and named Beverly Jean. She was quite the most flawless creature Kate had ever beheld in the movies or out.

To begin with, she had brown curls. A thick clump of them was held high on her head with a crisp blue bow. The rest swung and bobbed whenever Beverly Jean tossed her head, which was often. Her skin was fair and unblemished by a single freckle; her arms were dimpled and smooth; and she was dressed with costly care. Her blue eyes exactly matched her hair ribbon, and the lashes fringing them were long and black.

Kate had often in the past encountered scattered remnants of her ideal in one person or another. Met thus singly or in pairs, they had never failed to excite her admiration and had even caused her a twinge of envy now and then. But always she had been able to accept them more or less philosophically, that is to say, with good sense. Beverly Jean, however, was another matter. Here were all the scattered remnants brought together, each single one enhanced and made more glamor-

ous by its proximity to all the others. Here was the embodi-
ment of all Kate's longings, complete and perfect. As she
continued to stare, she knew such great and overwhelming
despair that it nearly sickened her.

To sit here and to see alive and off the screen the very thing
you most wanted to be and knew you never could be, was
enough to sicken anyone. Even a sensible person. Even a person who might someday be wise. "Someday" was away off in
the future, and Beverly Jean was here in the now.

Beverly Jean had spotted Kate almost as soon as she had
come into the room. Strangers were a constant source of delight to Beverly Jean. There was never any question of her
effect upon them. It was invariably flattering to herself. Kate
would perhaps have been interested to know that Beverly
Jean's ideas about charm were identical with her own and
her evaluation of them as high. Like Kate, she completely
believed that if you were pretty enough and cute enough,
everyone liked you and you could pretty much have your own
way in the world. But, unlike Kate, Beverly Jean enjoyed
the heady delight of knowing that she was certainly pretty
and, in all probability, cute.

So now she was pleasurably conscious of Kate's open admiration and was even prepared to react graciously to it. Her
most melting smile was beginning to deepen the dimple at
the corner of her mouth when something of the misery and
dismay Kate was feeling found their way into her face. Beverly Jean noticed the change instantly and unfortunately mis-
read it as uncomplimentary to herself.

Surprise rather than indignation stopped her in her tracks.

It was unthinkable! It was unbearable! It must be stopped! That anyone should dare to wear that look in the presence of Beverly Jean Brown, was like a slap in the face to her.

"It's rude to stare," said Beverly Jean coldly, staring back at Kate, a hard, disdainful stare.

Kate's eyes only widened, and her stare became more fixed. She knew that tone and she knew that look. That they should have their source in this peerless creature was so surprising that for a moment Kate was helpless. She could only continue to gaze into Beverly Jean's face, hoping desperately that she hadn't meant it, that perhaps it had been a joke. Kate had never known it was rude to stare.

If you were curious about a person, you simply continued to look at him until your curiosity was satisfied. Or so Kate had always thought. Cousin Ethel always had. One of her favorite boasts was that she never forgot a face. Of course, Cousin Ethel had sometimes proved an unreliable guide. However, like Cousin Ethel, Kate knew as her eyes held Beverly Jean's, that she would never forget this face. Anger was mounting in it, so she wasn't joking, as Kate had begun to hope. She really considered her, Kate, rude. It was a bad beginning and there was just one thing to be done about it.

"I'm sorry," said Kate, humbly. "I didn't know I was being rude."

As surely as ignorance is no excuse before the law, it proved to be no excuse in Beverly Jean's own particular code of justice. As to Kate's regret for her imperfect behavior, Beverly Jean chose to ignore that completely. So that the only reward Kate received for her effort to make amends was an indignant toss of her head as Beverly Jean flounced into her seat. Three girls who had been interested spectators in the little drama immediately leaned comfortingly toward Beverly Jean with sympathetic murmurs, accompanied by dark looks thrown in Kate's direction.

Kate, sitting forlorn and hopeless, knew with bitter certainty that she had made an enemy where more than anything else she had desired a friend. Next to looking like her ideal, would be the satisfaction of having a friend who looked like it. It was clear that all the other girls felt that way, too. Probably they would all be down on her now for having offended their favorite. If only she could manage somehow to make them understand that she hadn't intended to! That she hadn't meant to be rude. Hadn't even known it was rude to stare.

Strangely enough, it never occurred to Kate that Beverly Jean had been rude. It was all a part of her logic that the Beverly Jeans of this world were a law unto themselves. If you were pretty enough and cute enough, nothing else mattered. And Beverly Jean was both.

Feeling very much out of things, Kate began looking around the room. There was nothing else for her to do and she had to look somewhere, anywhere, that wasn't in the direction of Beverly Jean and her sympathizers.

Schoolrooms were pretty much alike, she decided, and, feeling unhappy, was unnecessarily irritated at the discovery. This one had a tiresome number of red hearts on display everywhere in it. They formed a border above the blackboards and were stuck all over the big box that Miss Morgan had been busy with.

Couldn't they think of anything besides hearts, she wondered? Then she remembered. This was St. Valentine's Day! Naturally, they would have to use hearts for St. Valentine's Day. Cupids were too hard to draw. It would have to be hearts, of course. But still, she decided irritably, there were too many of them.

Her restless gaze kept wandering about the room, falling at last on the wide window sill near Miss Morgan's desk. There it stopped. An aquarium! A nice, square, clean aquarium with rocks and with green things floating in it. Kate rose at once and went to the window. As she leaned over the aquarium, three tiny turtles jerked their heads part way back into their shells, then slowly let them glide forth again, the skin unwrinkling on the sides of their necks as their necks lengthened. Three heads turned sideways to look at Kate with coldly blinking eyes.

They're begging, she thought, and wished she had something to give them. The room didn't seem so silly now that she had discovered the turtles. If there had to be hearts, it was comforting to know there were turtles, too. For the moment, they even made her forget Beverly Jean.

Miss Morgan's voice, raised above the murmur of the room, recalled Kate to her seat.

"Will you please put your valentines in the post box?" she said.

Instantly, there was a rush to the front of the room where

the children began stuffing envelopes into the top of the decorated box. Kate knew these were valentines and she knew also that she would not be receiving any. Nor did she feel in any way left out on this account. A new person couldn't reasonably expect to have any. They didn't even know her name!

While the others were busy at the front of the room, Miss Morgan called Kate to her desk, asked her a lot of questions, and entered her name in her record book. By the time the business was finished, all the boys and girls had returned to their seats and were waiting for the next thing to happen.

"Boys and girls," said Miss Morgan, "this is Kate Summers and she is going to be in our room for good."

Miss Morgan sounded as if that were something very nice and Kate was just beginning to take a little satisfaction at her sudden place in the spotlight, when Beverly Jean Brown's hand shot into the air.

"Yes, Beverly Jean," said Miss Morgan, patiently, nodding to Kate that she might go to her seat.

"We have a new Buick with white-walled tires," announced Beverly Jean.

"So what?" asked a voice from the other side of the room in tones of utter disgust.

"Why, Vic," exclaimed Miss Morgan, "I'm ashamed of you. What will Kate think of us?"

Kate was already rapidly making up her mind about that, and she had already picked out Vic. He had black hair and snapping black eyes and he looked quite a lot like the kind of person who makes things happen. He was apparently not too impressed with the beautiful Beverly Jean. Kate liked him.

"And now," continued Miss Morgan blandly, exactly as if nothing had happened, "we will select a postman and pass out the valentines."

"We want Beverly Jean," came a dutiful chorus from the group that had earlier sympathized with her over Kate's rudeness. Kate looked across at Beverly Jean's perfect profile and wondered how they could want anyone else.

"Aw, she gets to do everything," came Vic's voice again. "Why can't the new girl be postman? She won't get any valentines anyway because she's new and it would be more fun for her than just sitting there watching us get ours."

Instantly Beverly Jean was on her feet. "She doesn't know our names and might call the wrong ones," she protested.

Kate, watching with interest this disposal of her person, could see reason in Beverly Jean's argument. And yet, she reminded herself, she was ten years old and knew how to read.

"I think Vic's suggestion is a very good one," said Miss Morgan, "and if Kate has trouble with the names, we can help her. Can't we, Beverly Jean?"

But Beverly Jean was looking down at her desk and said nothing. Again, the little girls were murmuring their sympathies and casting dark looks in Kate's direction.

"Would you like to be postman?" Miss Morgan asked her.

Kate looked doubtfully across at Vic, caught his grin and nod, and answered, "Yes, I'd like to."

So Kate passed out the valentines. She did stumble over a few names, but whenever this happened, Vic prompted her even before Miss Morgan could, Beverly Jean and her satellites only giggling rudely. But no one paid any attention to them.

Everyone appeared to have about an equal number, with Beverly Jean having a slight edge over all the rest by the time Kate got to the bottom of the box. Now there were just two envelopes in it. She picked up one of them. "Kate Summers," she read out loud, not realizing she had called her own name until Vic shouted with a great good-natured laugh, "That's you." It was the truth. So unexpectedly had her own name appeared, that Kate hadn't even recognized it. She smiled a little shyly, turning the envelope over and over in her hands.

"Open it," commanded Vic impatiently, and Kate did.

The whole class watched her as she drew out of the envelope a valentine picturing a little girl with red pigtails standing on a cliff with the sea behind her and a gull wheeling over her shoulder. There was a word dangling from each pigtail and one word said "Sensible" and the other said "Kate." Below ran the following: "Please be our valentine." It didn't say anything more, but Kate knew who had sent it. Christopher and Nora, of course. She laughed out loud it was such a funny valentine.

"Who's it from?" demanded Vic, and before she had time to remember that it was really none of his business, Kate answered, "Christopher and Nora Cline." Vic looked pleased, but said nothing.

As Kate put the valentine back into its envelope, she caught a whisper from Beverly Jean's side of the room. "Homemade," she heard, and there was another giggle. Without let-

ting on she had overheard, Kate reached for the last remaining valentine. This time she really looked at the name before reading it out.

"It's for me," she said to Miss Morgan.

It was a very large envelope and when Kate carefully drew the valentine out of its cover, its beauty made her gasp. First of all, there were two hands clasped beneath a dove in flight. Then there was a lace paper frame which stood out like a little window when you pulled up a cardboard hinge. And last and most wonderful of all, were the words "St. Valentine" written in narrow blue ribbon across the top. Kate carefully turned it over and read on the back: "We are glad you are our valentine." Who could have sent it? Why, Mr. and Mrs. Tuttle, of course.

Kate looked triumphantly toward Beverly Jean. She knew no one else had received such a handsome valentine as this. But Beverly Jean was intensely interested at that moment in something under her desk. So, a bit crestfallen, Kate returned to her seat.

Off and on for the rest of the school day, Kate thought about Beverly Jean. She thought about her more than about anything else, because Beverly Jean troubled her. To begin with, she didn't seem pleased no matter what happened, and the more people tried to please her, the harder she was to satisfy. Had Kate been a little more sensible, she might have wondered why anybody tried. She did go so far, however, as to wonder whether being pretty was, after all, sufficient reason for being happy. Because obviously, Beverly Jean wasn't. Else why didn't she ever smile? It seemed to Kate that she should have been the happiest person under the sun. But unless she was talking to Miss Morgan or someone was saying something pleasant about her dress or her hair or something she had done, Beverly Jean's face wore a perpetual pout.

Not that Beverly Jean ever did very much. She spent most of her time explaining why she couldn't. Her recitations were certainly nothing for her to brag about, Kate noticed. But, at recess, Kate learned that she was a "marvelous tap dancer," and Kate was sure again that this, coupled with her good looks, was all she needed. And then, of course, there was the Buick with white-walled tires. Reading and writing and arithmetic seemed suddenly very unimportant beside tap dancing and cuteness and cars. Again, Kate experienced that pang of despair she had felt on first beholding Beverly Jean. If only she herself could have been cute instead of merely sensible!

Before the school day ended, Beverly Jean made an announcement. She did it very importantly, standing up in front of the class and Kate thought what a fine thing it would be to stand like that in front of the whole class making an announcement of your very own, just as if you were the teacher. Beverly Jean was inviting all the class to her birthday party the following Saturday.

"I want everybody to come, even Vic Corsatti and the new girl," she said.

Kate knew very well that being singled out like this for special mention was by no means a compliment. Quite the opposite, in fact. She heard Vic's derisive snort and she made up her mind then and there that she would not be among those present at Beverly Jean's party.

"It's to be a theater party," Beverly Jean went on. "We will all meet at two o'clock at the Strand Theater and after the show we'll all go to my house for refreshments."

It sounded alluring, all right. Kate hadn't been to a movie for quite a while. She wouldn't have to talk to Beverly Jean during the picture, she suddenly realized. Afterward might not be so bad, either. Maybe Beverly Jean hadn't meant to be unkind, after all. Maybe this was just her way of saying, "I'm sorry."

Kate watched hopefully as Beverly Jean bustled importantly to her seat, her smile more smug than gracious at the appreciative murmur which rose about her. But there was no forgiving smile thrown in Kate's direction and she was forced to admit that she had only been fooling herself. Beverly Jean hated her just as surely as she hated Vic Corsatti. And for no good reason. That there was a standing quarrel between her and Vic there could be no doubt and the reason was obvious. Vic refused to be impressed by her. But there was no quarrel between Kate and Beverly Jean. Only a misunderstanding, and it had come about because Kate *had* been impressed by her. It was all most regrettable. But there was no use getting around it, Kate simply couldn't be expected to go to the party. And she imagined that Beverly Jean would be relieved rather than hurt by her absence.

After school, Kate started alone across the school grounds, trying not to hear Beverly Jean's too loud good-bys as she climbed into the new car which was waiting for her, complete with white-walled tires and Beverly Jean's mother. Kate didn't look up as it purred past her along the street and out of sight.

"You got the best valentines."

Kate turned to see Vic Corsatti hurrying to catch up with her. "How come you know Chris?" he asked, falling into step beside her.

"Christopher and Nora are old friends of mine," explained Kate airily. "I've known them ever since yesterday morning."

"That's nothin'," returned Vic, "I've known 'em ever since last year when they first came here."

"I even helped Nora clean house," Kate offered, with the look of one who has scored.

"That's nothin'," said Vic again. "They eat at our house lots and go out with Leo in the boat."

"Oh," said Kate, searching her mind for something that would top this. There was the secret, of course, but it was unthinkable to mention that. It was a secret. Then there was the memory of Nora's tears. She'd bet Vic had never seen Nora cry. But somehow a friend's grief didn't seem the sort of thing you could display like a kind of trophy. That was a secret, too, she realized, just as much a secret as if it had been labeled one.

"Who is Leo?" she asked at length, hoping to turn the conversation into safer channels.

"My brother," said Vic in a voice so full of pride you could fairly hear trumpets sounding through it. "My big brother

70

and he's one swell guy. He's six feet high and he ain't afraid of anything. And he's the best fisherman in the bay. And he's sure good to me."

Kate looked at Vic and saw his face shining with such devotion that she looked away quickly as if she had witnessed something she had no right to see. Something private and holy.

"You like him a lot, don't you?" she said lamely, feeling it a very inadequate response to that look, but unable to think of anything better at the moment.

"*Like* him?" repeated Vic scornfully. "He's my brother Leo." Again that ringing pride, that special look.

Kate was impressed. None of her cousins had ever spoken of one another in this way. Leo must be a very special person.

At Lighthouse Avenue, Vic said, "Well, so long. Be seein' you."

"But that's the street the Clines live on," said Kate.

"Any law against my livin' on it, too?" Vic's eyes were teasing her. "I knew you'd been over yesterday. Christopher gave me that valentine to take to you. We had it all planned for you to be postman."

"Beverly Jean was awfully mad," said Kate.

"Forget it," advised Vic. "She's always mad about something and taking it out on somebody. Christopher says beauties have been like that since the dawn of history. He says it's the price we have to pay for envying them."

"Do you envy Beverly Jean?" demanded Kate in astonishment. Vic seemed to have too much good sense for that.

"Gosh, no," he said quickly. "She gives me a pain with all her bragging and stuck-up ways."

"Are you going to her party?" asked Kate.

"Sure. Everybody does. Are you?"

"I'm not sure," answered Kate cautiously. She had decided to have a little talk with Nora before she definitely made up her mind.

They said good-by and Kate walked very slowly the rest of the way home. "It's the price you pay for envying them." Beverly Jean had made her miserable today. But did she envy her? Not even such beauty as hers was a guarantee of people's liking, Kate had discovered, for neither she nor Vic liked Beverly Jean. But did she envy her? Kate got almost to the Tuttle front door before she was able to face honestly her own answer to her own question. And the answer was anything but sensible. Yes, there was no getting around it, she did.

Chapter V

Scent of Cedar

WHEN Kate got inside the Tuttle house, she laid her valentines carefully on the chair in the tiny hall before slipping off her coat. The sight of them lying there as she reached into the closet for a hanger presented to Kate a fresh problem which at the moment had power to banish even such a baffling and beautiful enigma as Beverly Jean from the forefront of her mind.

She was going to have to thank Mr. Tuttle for his share in one of them, and she was beginning to wonder mightily just how it was going to be done. Would he come out from behind his newspaper long enough for her to do it? It was becoming impossible for her to think of Mr. Tuttle without seeing simultaneously long columns of fine print. As a matter of fact, except for what Mrs. Tuttle had happened to say about him, Mr. Tuttle was as much a mystery on this second evening at his house as he had been, right at the start.

Kate stood for a moment in the hall, fingering the valentines and wondering why this should be so. Why did Mr. Tuttle seem not to want to talk to her? Did he perhaps not like her? Of course she was too homely for anyone to like right off and he had given her no opportunity to prove that she was sensible. On the other hand, Nora and Christopher seemed not to dislike her and they were grown-ups, too. But then, they had learned almost at once about her good sense. In fact, it was on the strength of it that she had been asked to their house. How could she make Mr. Tuttle recognize it, too?

Pondering this, she moved in the direction of the kitchen from which sounds of Mrs. Tuttle at the business of getting dinner were vigorously emanating. You could almost count on Mrs. Tuttle's being busy with either cooking, cleaning, or mending. After just two days, Kate was already beginning to wonder why Mrs. Tuttle never did anything else.

Just sitting idly in her presence seemed a kind of social error. Maybe that was the reason that Mr. Tuttle always held a newspaper up in front of him. It made him appear to be doing something. It was rather a pity, Kate thought, that Mrs. Tuttle and Nora couldn't share their respective merits and lacks in the way of housekeeping. Between them, they'd strike a nice balance.

"Oh, there you are," said Mrs. Tuttle welcomingly as Kate appeared in the kitchen doorway. "How did things go to-day?"

"I got two valentines," said Kate.

"You did!" exclaimed Mrs. Tuttle, looking a little too surprised.

"One of them was from Christopher and Nora and one was from you and Mr. Tuttle," replied Kate. "Yours was the prettiest one in the whole room."

Mrs. Tuttle slipped a roast into the oven, thereby hiding

a pleased face from Kate. "Why, I don't know what you're talking about," she said. "Valentines were supposed to be a mystery when I was a little girl. You never can be sure who sent them."

"I'm sure," said Kate firmly. "And I thank you."

Mrs. Tuttle said nothing but handed Kate a pan of potatoes to peel.

"You can sit down here at the table and do them or stand up at the sink," she said. "I'd like them cut lengthwise, so I can bake them in the pan with the meat. You can get an apron out of that bottom drawer."

Kate put the valentines on the table and got the apron. Standing at the sink as she peeled the potatoes, being careful to dig out every single eye, she had plenty of time to review the day's events. Some of them she recounted for Mrs. Tuttle, but she was careful to withhold all mention of Beverly Jean. She didn't want her to know she had made an enemy, perhaps several enemies since Beverly Jean had friends, on this her first day at school. Instead, she talked at some length about Vic Corsatti.

"He lives on the same street as Christopher and Nora. I know because we walked home together."

"The Corsattis are fisher-folk," said Mrs. Tuttle. "Vic's the baby of the family and a little spoiled, I've always thought. His brothers and sisters have let him do about as he pleased ever since he was born. Especially Leo. Leo's the best of the whole lot in my opinion and they're all mighty fine people. I'm glad you've got acquainted with Vic. You'll be company for each other."

75

When she had finished with the potatoes, Mrs. Tuttle gave Kate some carrots to scrape. "I'm going to cook them in the oven, too," she explained. "Whenever I have a roast, I try to get my whole dinner cooked with it. It saves on fuel."

Kate thought this a very sensible plan and made a mental note of it to share with Nora some time when the right moment should present itself. She had an idea that Nora didn't know the first thing about saving fuel, and since Christopher was obviously hard up, the knowledge might be useful.

After the carrots were scraped, Kate set the table, then, there being nothing more for her to do until the dinner was served, she put on her coat and went outside.

From the safety of her own front steps, she looked over at the house with the cactus. It looked even gloomier at this hour of the day than it had yesterday morning. A rising wind moved the limbs of the old cypress and one of them creaked dismally as it rubbed against the roof of the porch.

While Kate stood there, the front door opened and an old woman came out on the porch. She closed the door carefully behind her, then came slowly down the steps. She had a bucket with a rope tied to the handle in one of her hands. She was stooped and dressed all in black, and she looked almost as broad as she did tall. Her full skirt swung about her ankles as she walked down the path, muttering something which Kate couldn't hear.

Her face was almost hidden under the down-turned brim of an old black straw hat, but Kate could easily imagine from the general look of her that it wasn't a pleasant face. And what on earth was she doing with a bucket that had a rope tied to its handle? All at once, she looked over at Kate and came to a full stop.

"Are you living there or just visiting?" she asked, tipping back her head to see out from under the hat brim. Her face was definitely unpleasant. Even unfriendly.

"I'm living here, I guess," answered Kate, her heart suddenly beating faster. There was something a little fearsome about this old woman.

"Well, be mighty careful that you don't bother me or Timothy," said the old woman. "Just stay where you belong."

"Who's Timothy?" asked Kate, wondering if any child could be so unfortunate as to have to live in that house with this person.

"Timothy is my cat," came the reply, "and he doesn't like children any better than I do."

"So I was right all along," thought Kate. "She doesn't like children. I just knew it."

Without saying more, the old woman swung around and went on down the walk, turning seaward when she reached the street. Kate watched her out of sight while curiosity, foreboding, and frank amazement fought for first place in her mind.

After a while, Mr. Tuttle came home. Kate watched him hurrying up the street looking smaller than ever in his overcoat. He said hello to her, hesitated as if he might say more, then fled up the steps and into the house. There hadn't been any chance at all for mentioning the valentine.

"I guess he doesn't like me," Kate said out loud, her eyes following him. She said it without rancor, as one might say,

"I guess it will rain tonight." Well, there was nothing she could do about it, she decided. In time, when Mr. Tuttle had had a chance to notice her good sense, he might change his feeling toward her. In the meantime, she would have to continue just minding her p's and q's, doing what was expected of her, and hoping for the best. If that didn't work, the county would find another place for her. You couldn't expect, of course, that anyone would want a child around for long whom he didn't like. Such an arrangement wouldn't make sense.

Just before dinner and out of a clear blue sky, as it were, Mrs. Tuttle suggested that Kate run upstairs and comb her hair.

"Don't bother to unbraid it," she said, "just smooth the top a bit. Red hair looks so wild when it gets tousled."

Surprised, Kate went dutifully to her room, cautiously feeling the top of her head as she went. It felt as smooth as usual and, a moment later, the mirror revealed no tousled state. But just the same, Kate passed the comb from the part in the middle to the braid at each side. Then she returned to the kitchen.

As she passed by the dinner table, something upon it caught her eye. She tried to continue on her way, but it was impossible. She simply had to stop and look, for there, set squarely at her place, was a rather long and somewhat narrow package. It was a box because its corners were square and she was sure it hadn't been there before she went upstairs. It wasn't wrapped prettily. It wore nothing gayer than

78

stout manila paper with string around it. But had it been decked out in tinsel it couldn't have cried, "Present," more plainly.

Kate's usually grave eyes were almost dancing when at last she sat at the table with Mr. Tuttle inviting her to open her gift. "It's for you and I hope you'll like it," he said. Then, looking a little apprehensively at Mrs. Tuttle, he added, "It's a very useful thing and you really need it."

As she untied the string, there were two thoughts uppermost in Kate's mind. One was that Mr. Tuttle couldn't dislike her very much if he was giving her a present, and the second was, what thing could it be that she badly needed? She had long wanted some patent leather slippers, but they would make a bigger bundle than this. And she didn't really need them, anyway, since her feet were adequately if not beautifully shod in a strong pair of useful and sensible ones, the only kind the county purchasing agent would allow. What would the box hold? This suspense was delightful and she half-hoped it would last forever even while she speeded her already eager fingers.

At last the wrapping fell away. There stood the box all right, just as Kate had suspected. It was a neat little box made of wood, and it had a lid which she now lifted carefully. But the box was empty! Completely empty! She closed the lid, biting back her disappointment as she realized what her gift was. It was a pencil box! Nothing more nor less. Just a pencil box! Kate studied the bright picture pasted on its cover while she chewed her lip and determined that the tears swimming in her eyes should not fall. She had looked forward to something really nice, and it had turned out to be nothing but a pencil box.

Nobody used them nowadays. You were a sissy if you did. The picture showed two deer drinking at a narrow stream at sunset. There was a green forest all about them. The deer were brown and the sunset very red. Kate cared nothing about the deer or the sunset. They were silly like the stupid box which wasn't good for anything.

"When I was a little boy," Kate tried to listen to what Mr. Tuttle was saying, grateful that for the moment she would not have to speak. "When I was a little boy," he repeated, "we used to start each new school year with a new pencil box. That is, if we got promoted we did." He chuckled quietly like someone remembering something. "It was always a fine thing, having a new pencil box. They were made of cedar, usually, and when you opened them, you could smell the cedar plain. It was like having a little forest sitting on your desk. And the pictures on the top made you think of places lots pleasanter than the school rooms I used to sit in. Of course now it's different. Schools are better places than they were when I was a little boy. But still, I thought it might smell good to you sometimes to get a whiff of cedar. This box isn't real cedar, but I made the clerk hunt up some cedar dust to shake into it and we left some of the crumbs in so it'd smell good to you."

Kate had been listening with her eyes glued to the pencil box and she had been thinking hard. Mr. Tuttle apparently didn't know that children didn't care about such things nowadays. He was *old*. It must be nearly fifty years since Mr. Tuttle was a little boy. Why, fifty years was half a century. How could he possibly understand what children were like today?

"I grew up in the Middle West. There were hardly any trees around anywhere," he continued. "It used to be mighty good to open the box, shut your eyes, and smell the clean smell of cedar. You could start right off imagining you were in deep woods with bears and Indians, maybe."

He chuckled again and Kate looked at him. He was staring into his plate, but she knew he wasn't seeing it. She knew he was looking back along all those years since he was a little boy and there was homesickness in his face. It was funny to think of Mr. Tuttle as a little boy imagining a pencil box into a forest full of Indians. But he had been that little boy just as she, Kate, was now, at this very moment, a little girl. Would she remember half a century from now how sorry she had been to receive a pencil box?

"Don't think I've ever heard you talk so much since we were married," declared Mrs. Tuttle, passing her husband the potatoes. "It's wonderful the way a youngster loosens tongues. But I guess the cat got Kate's."

For Kate was still thinking. A gift. Mr. Tuttle had meant to surprise her and to please her. Evidently he did like her a little, after all. She opened the box again and now noticed for the first time the strong scent of cedar that floated up to her. It *was* a woodsy smell. It was as if the forest on the cover had come alive. "It was like having a little forest of your own on your desk," Mr. Tuttle had said.

What would the others think? What would Beverly Jean say? Suddenly, Kate knew that she didn't care what Beverly Jean said. This was her pencil box, her very own. She would take it to school and when she lifted the cover and smelled the cedar, she would think of a little boy who had once smelled the same smell in a place called the Middle West and who had remembered it always, just as she would.

"It's a beautiful pencil box and I want to use it all the rest of the way through school," Kate said with honest thankfulness.

Mr. Tuttle gave her his funny little smile and Mrs. Tuttle said, "Eat your dinner, now. It's getting all cold."

After the dinner dishes are done, Kate asked for permission to go over to the Clines'.

"I don't know about that," said Mrs. Tuttle doubtfully. "You were there only yesterday. Why don't you just stay here this evening and look at magazines? I've got a whole stack of them that ought to be sorted and you could do it for me."

Kate could think of nothing she would enjoy less at the moment than sorting magazines, for there was a problem troubling her, a problem which she was certain only Nora could solve.

"Oh, let her go, Martha," said Mr. Tuttle, surprisingly. "The Clines are sensible young people. If they don't want her, they'll send her home. A cat in a strange garret is always restless."

They exchanged glances, the little man and the little girl. Hers was grateful, his understanding. In that moment, there was born to them an appreciation of each other's positions and of what it meant to be a little girl in a strange house and a foster parent of a strange little girl. From that moment, Kate was never to doubt Mr. Tuttle again, and from that moment, he, in his turn, was to be her open and declared champion. From that evening, Mrs. Tuttle, for all the respect and affection they were both to accord her, was to find herself ever after a lone individual pitted against a closed and secret society, the membership of which was composed of just two people, Mr. Tuttle and Kate.

As Kate stepped outside, she buttoned her coat about her. The wind, instead of dying at sunset, had strengthened and swept up the street from the sea. She could smell the rain in it. The bare branches of the walnut tree clicked against each other over her head as she walked beneath them to the sidewalk. There, the wind fairly blew her along the street to Lighthouse Avenue. She saw a light glowing in the Cline house and began to run. Mrs. Tuttle had said she couldn't stay more than an hour and she had no time to waste.

It was Christopher who opened the door to her. Kate was just a little disappointed at seeing him, for what she had to discuss was strictly a feminine matter, and she doubted his ability to understand. Christopher considered her sensible and the thing on her mind concerned Beverly Jean Brown. Already Kate realized that it was practically impossible for her to be sensible where Beverly Jean was concerned. She couldn't bear the thought of having Christopher think her silly.

But his first words put her mind at ease. "I'm glad to see you," he said, helping her off with her coat. Nora hailed her from the sofa, uncurling herself like a freshly awakened kit-

83

ten. "I was going over to Corsatti's for a little while and now Nora will have company."

"I'm glad," said Kate. "I came especially to see Nora."

"Then I won't clutter up the scene another moment," and hauling a sweater over his head and grinning over his shoulder at Nora, Christopher disappeared forthwith into the night.

"Now, what's on your mind?" asked Nora, throwing a pillow at the other end of the sofa and motioning Kate toward it.

"Did you ever hear of Beverly Jean Brown?" asked Kate.

"Heavens, yes," answered Nora. "She's the wonder child of the village."

Kate let this pass as a plain statement of simple truth.

"She's giving a birthday party next Saturday and she's invited the whole class."

Nora looked steadily at Kate. "You're going, of course."

"That's what I came to see you about," said Kate. "I don't want to."

"Why?"

"Beverly Jean doesn't like me."

"Why?"

"I stared at her and it made her mad."

"Hm-m-m-m," said Nora. "First time I ever heard of her objecting to that."

"She said it was rude to stare."

"It is," said Nora, "but it hardly makes sense for the pot to call the kettle black. Beverly Jean's manners are not too perfect."

"She's awful pretty," said Kate.

"I'm terribly tempted to say 'handsome is as handsome does.' There, I've said it anyway," declared Nora.

"And I don't like her," Kate confessed, bringing the conversation back to the main problem. "So you see why I don't want to go to her party."

"Well, you'll have to go anyway," said Nora, "and for two reasons. First, to stay away would place your manners on a par with hers, and that would be terrible. Secondly, it would make you seem as eager for the spotlight as Beverly Jean. Your absence would be noted and misconstrued. You're not the type, Kate."

Kate sat quietly for a moment, twisting her fingers in her lap. Then she said, still looking down at her fingers, "If you go to a birthday party, you have to take a present, don't you?"

Nora, too, was silent for a moment before she said, "You're supposed to, I believe."

"Well, I haven't anything to take and I can't ask the Tuttles for anything because they just gave me a valentine and a pencil box and besides I haven't been there long enough."

The ticking of the alarm clock on the mantel became positively noisy before Nora spoke again. At last she asked, "I don't suppose you would care to give her the pencil box?"

Kate looked up quickly. "Oh, I couldn't," she said. "It was a present from Mr. Tuttle. He'd think I didn't like it and I do." Kate went on to describe the pencil box with what for her amounted to extraordinary enthusiasm.

Nora nodded. "I see," she said. "Of course you couldn't."

There was another long silence. Kate could hear the precious seconds ticking into eternity. Almost half an hour had passed and the greatest part of the problem still remained to be solved.

All at once, Nora snapped her fingers and sat bolt upright. "I've got it," she cried, and was off the sofa and across the room before Kate could recover from her start. She began rooting into a cupboard, hurling things out behind her until she had half buried herself in its dark recesses. Finally she emerged, her hair down over her flushed face, and a little wooden box in her hand.

"Look," she cried. "It's a miniature cedar chest. Chris got it for me once full of candy and it was so sweet I saved it. We're going to make a pencil box out of this for Beverly Jean."

It was a dear little cedar chest, Kate thought, exactly like the big ones she had seen in furniture store windows. But it was too wide for a proper pencil box. She said so quite frankly.

"I know that," Nora replied. "But we can cut it down. Chris has a fret saw and I'm rather good at such things. Much better than I am at painting," she added as if to reassure Kate.

Kate still wasn't enthusiastic. "But you'd be doing all the work," she protested.

"Oh no," said Nora. "We'd ask Christopher to paint a picture for the cover. He'd be glad to, I know."

"That isn't what I mean," explained Kate. "I wouldn't be having anything to do with it."

86

Nora crossed over to the sofa and sat down, the little box nestling in her lap. "I see," she said softly. She reached out and took one of Kate's hands in hers. "Did you ever owe anyone for anything, Kate?" she asked, surprisingly. Nora was certainly a most unexpected person. Kate shook her head.

"I've always helped with the housework," she said.

"Then," continued Nora, "you have no idea how Christopher and I feel about what you did for us yesterday."

Kate looked at her in astonishment. "You mean helping you to clean the house?"

"That and more," replied Nora.

"But that was fun," cried Kate. "I didn't expect anything for it."

"I know you didn't," said Nora, "but just the same, you helped me a lot. And now in return it is only fair to let me help you. It's the very least you can do in all decency, Kate. It's the sensible thing, really."

Kate turned this over in her mind very carefully. The more she thought about it, the more it seemed to make sense. "Turn about is fair play," Cousin Ethel had often said. This was certainly turn about. In a way, it would be her own gift, after all. Just as much as if she had bought it in a store.

"All right," said Kate. "I'll come by for it Saturday morning. That gives you three days."

"Loads of time," said Nora. "And now tell me how school went today. You can skip Beverly Jean. She bores me."

"Oh," said Kate, all at once remembering. "I forgot to thank Christopher and you for the valentine. I liked it."

"He had a lot of fun doing it," said Nora. "Tell me, how do you like Vic?"

"He's O.K." declared Kate.

"The whole family is," said Nora. "Wait until you meet Leo. He's almost as nice as Christopher."

The hour was nearly up when Christopher came home. "Grab your coat," he said to Kate, "I'll take you across to the Tuttles'."

At the door, Nora bent over and kissed Kate on the forehead. "Sleep tight," she said.

With heads bent against the wind and with hands deep in coat pockets, Kate and Christopher walked the three blocks to the Tuttles' in silence. At the porch steps, she thanked him for the valentine and his company. Then they said good-night and Kate climbed the steps. As she opened the front door, a flood of warm light spread for a moment across the porch, silhouetting her figure against it and making her red head fairly glow. Christopher stood watching her, hunched against the wind, until she shut the door behind her. Then he plodded cheerfully home to Nora.

Later, when Kate washed her face and hands before getting into bed, she was very careful to wash around the spot where Nora's lips had touched her.

Chapter VI

Kate Changes the Pattern

SATURDAY was cleaning day at the Tuttles', so on this first Saturday morning Kate stood in the middle of the living-room, dust rag in hand, trying to decide where she had left off and feeling certain that she had dusted every chair twice just to be on the safe side. As she had suspected, cleaning for Mrs. Tuttle was no fun at all. Things looked no better after you had finished than they had before, because everything was spotless in the beginning. The only thing that could be said for Saturday morning so far, was that on this day Mrs. Tuttle also did her baking and now the heady odor of cookies came to mingle with the clean smell of furniture polish and floor wax.

It was a tantalizing spring day. Wednesday night's wind had brought two days of rain, but now it was clear, and the sunlight warming the window ledges held no hint of winter in it.

Leaning from an open window after shaking her dust cloth out of it, Kate looked up into the blue sky and thought what a fine day it was for a birthday party. Beverly Jean certainly had all the luck! She lowered her gaze to the general direction of Christopher's house, wondering without any real concern whether the pencil box was ready. Nora wouldn't let her down. She'd run over to get it as soon as she had finished with the cleaning. She was about to draw in her head and shut the window when she saw Vic come around the corner from Lighthouse Avenue. He waved frantically as he caught sight of her, so she settled herself on the window sill once more to wait for him.

"Hello," he said, as he reached the house. "Whatcha doing?"

"Cleaning," answered Kate.

Vic sniffed suddenly. "Something sure smells good."

"Mrs. Tuttle's baking cookies."

"When did she start?"

"About half an hour ago. I guess by the smell that the first pan's come out of the oven."

"I bet they sure taste good," suggested Vic.

"I haven't tasted them yet," replied Kate.

There was a silence loud with unspoken speech. Then Vic said, "I had my breakfast kinda early. A couple of cookies would taste good."

"Yes, I guess they would," said Kate.

There was another silence during which Vic scowled fiercely at nothing more important than his own two feet.

"If you'll snag a couple of those cookies for me, I'll let you go over to the wharf with me some day to meet Leo."

Kate swung the dust rag back and forth. "I couldn't do that," she said.

"I'll take you this afternoon," offered Vic.

"I'm going to Beverly Jean's party," said Kate.

"That's right," answered Vic. "I'd forgotten. So am I."

Suddenly Vic said, after a long interval of what must have been painful thought, "If you'll get me two of those cookies, I'll let you be my girl friend."

Kate stopped swinging the dust rag back and forth. "What does that mean?" she asked.

"Oh," said Vic, kicking at an imaginary rock, "it just means that I always stick up for you and maybe some day I'll get Leo to take you out in the boat."

Kate thought this over. Vic had already stood up for her once and she had been glad he did. To know that she could depend on his backing in future would by no means be unpleasant. Already he seemed a rather special friend of hers since he had walked home from school with her and since they shared in common the friendship of Christopher and Nora. Certainly the possibility of some day going out in the boat with Leo was most attractive. Yes, viewed from every angle, the prospect of being Vic Corsatti's girl friend seemed altogether agreeable and sensible.

"All right," said Kate, at last. "You wait here. I'll go and see what I can do."

She left the window, then turned back to say, "It may take quite a while. Don't go away."

"I won't," promised Vic, and Kate departed toward the kitchen.

She went slowly, trying to formulate a plan. She might come right out and ask Mrs. Tuttle, but suppose she should say, "No"? Mrs. Tuttle had never said "No" outright to the few favors Kate had asked of her so far. But there was sure to be a first time one of these days. This was not the time to hazard it, certainly.

Now Kate stood in the kitchen looking with longing eyes at the table spread temptingly with the first pan of cookies warm and crisp and smelling of sugar and vanilla.

"All finished?" asked Mrs. Tuttle pleasantly, as she slid the second pan into the oven.

"I think so," said Kate, eying the cookies pointedly. Mrs. Tuttle seemed not to notice.

Cousin Ethel had never bothered to bake cookies. She always said you could get them at the bakery for less than the trouble they cost you. But she never got as many as this, nor did they ever look so delicious.

"Did you remember to wipe behind the Chesterfield?" asked Mrs. Tuttle. Would she never get her mind off the cleaning, Kate wondered.

"Yes," she said. Then, "Isn't it a lot of trouble to make cookies?"

"Trouble? Gracious no. Simplest baking in the world. I'll show you how one of these days, then we can take turns with the cleaning and the baking."

At another time, Kate would have enjoyed contemplating this possibility and its wider implications. Evidently Mrs. Tuttle expected her to be with them for quite a little while, at least. But Vic was waiting on the front steps, and Kate knew enough about boys like Vic to know that he wouldn't wait forever. How *could* she manage to get a couple of those cookies?

"Now," said Mrs. Tuttle, "let's go in and see what kind of a housekeeper you are."

Kate's heart fell, but she followed her patiently into the living-room. There, Mrs. Tuttle with the eye of an expert, inspected every corner. But an expert had already been at work on every corner so she found nothing to complain of. She moved a chair or two, straightened a picture, then turned to Kate.

"I couldn't have done a better job myself," she said. "In fact, I'm so well pleased with what you've done that I'm going to give you a bag of cookies and turn you loose for the rest of the morning. You won't even have to do the lunch dishes."

Mrs. Tuttle bustled out of the room without waiting to see how Kate would take this sudden turn of events. So she missed seeing Kate recover from her astonishment in time to give Vic a reassuring signal before she followed Mrs. Tuttle into the kitchen. The last thing Kate had expected was that she might receive any special reward for a job well done. You did things because it was expected of you and, for Kate, to do anything at all, was to do it to the best of her ability. She just happened to be made that way. It was pleasant, just the same, to have the fact recognized. And when, a few minutes later, she held out the bag of cookies to a grinning Vic, she was thinking that cleaning for Mrs. Tuttle was, after all and in its special way, as agreeable as cleaning for Nora had been.

Together, Kate and Vic went over to the Clines' to get Beverly Jean's birthday present.

"What did you give her?" asked Kate.

"My sister Lena picked out a handkerchief for her," Vic replied.

"Just think," said Kate, "she'll get thirty-eight presents if everyone in the class goes to her party."

"Thirty-nine, counting Miss Morgan," corrected Vic, "but they'll mostly be handkerchiefs."

"Handkerchiefs are always useful," said Kate primly.

"I guess they're all right for girls," returned Vic. "I never bother with 'em myself. Neither does Leo. Except for church," he added, just remembering.

As they approached the Clines' garden gate, they could smell the appetizing odor of frying onions. Even at this hour of the morning, ten-thirty to be exact, they smelled exceedingly good. Vic quickened his steps.

"They're having hamburgers," he said.

Like a veteran, he led Kate straight around to the back of the house where they found Christopher and Nora busy in the kitchen. They were eating hamburgers all right.

"Just in time," cried Nora, opening the back door to them. "How much meat have we left, Christopher? Vic's good for three."

"Only two this morning," said Vic, modestly. "I've just eaten four cookies."

"And you?" turning to Kate.

"I don't know," said Kate. "I never had hamburgers except at regular meal times."

"Well, don't look so righteous about it," said Christopher laughing. "Is there anything wrong with having them now?

And how do you know that this isn't our regular meal time?"

"I don't," returned Kate gravely. "But it seems sort of shiftless to be cooking so soon after breakfast."

"Don't be tiresome, Kate," warned Nora. "Christopher had his breakfast at six o'clock and has been out sketching all morning. He's ravenous. How many will you have?"

"One," said Kate. And as she downed it a few minutes later, she knew that no hamburger she had ever eaten at high noon had ever tasted better. Maybe there was something to be said for being just a little shiftless, after all.

After the mess had been more or less cleared away, Nora showed Kate the pencil box. It was at least ten times nicer than she had expected it would be. No one could have guessed that it had ever been intended for any other purpose than that of a pencil box. Nora had even made a little compartment at one end with a sliding wall for pens and erasers. And the picture which Christopher had painted for the cover showed a pine forest on a cliff above the sea. They had shellacked it so that the cover was as shiny as the one on Kate's and altogether it was in every way satisfactory. Kate was delighted and showed it. And when Nora produced some white tissue paper and pink ribbon together with a little card, Kate thought the day could hold no more in the way of happy surprises.

But that was where Kate was wrong. She could hardly have foreseen at this moment what a big surprise was lying in wait for her only a few hours away. Kate had changed one pattern by eating hamburgers at what she considered an unorthodox hour, and was none the worse for it. She was to change still another with equally satisfactory results. She was, in the hours ahead, to do something that was not expected of her. And she was going to enjoy the doing of it very much indeed. Beverly Jean's birthday was to prove as important to a certain little girl named Kate Summers as to Beverly Jean herself. Kate was to wonder, later, if it hadn't actually proved to be more important.

At one o'clock, Kate began getting ready for the party. Mrs. Tuttle had, of course, granted her approval several days ago. She had even asked about a present when Kate broached the subject to her.

"Nora and I have that all fixed up," Kate had answered.

"Thank goodness," Mrs. Tuttle had replied. "I'm thinking that Nora would know a whole lot more about what a little girl would like than I ever would. I'm afraid I don't know too much about them," she had added, somewhat wistfully.

Kate had withheld comment because she thought as Mrs. Tuttle did.

"But it isn't because I don't want to know," Mrs. Tuttle had said. "Perhaps if I try to remember how I used to feel when I was about your age, I'll do better."

"I guess little girls don't change much over the years," Kate had observed sagely, and they had both felt more comfortable about each other after that.

Promptly at two o'clock, Kate presented herself at the entrance of the Strand Theater. Several others of her classmates were already there, Vic among them. He had already found out that the newsreel was playing and that the feature didn't start until half past two. Kate was relieved because her favorite child actress was playing that day, the one whose hair-do Beverly Jean duplicated with such success. Before meeting Beverly Jean, this child actress had been Kate's ideal. Vic, however, was disappointed in the film.

"Why couldn't they have picked a Western?" he wanted to know, and several of the boys echoed his sentiments. "I'll sure be glad when that kid starts losing her teeth," he said.

"Why?" asked one of the girls.

"Because then she won't look pretty any more," he said, "and they won't have her in pictures."

"She has started to lose them," Kate put in, "but they do bridge work on her and put in false ones until the others grow back. I read about it in a movie magazine once when I was waiting for Cousin Ethel at a beauty parlor."

"Oh," said Vic, accepting Kate's statement without question. There could be no appeal from a movie magazine.

After about fifteen minutes, Beverly Jean and her mother with Miss Morgan and another woman arrived in all the splendor of white-walled tires, and after only a brief delay during which Beverly Jean received the greetings of everyone not too self-conscious to voice them, they all began to file into the theater.

Two rows of seats had been reserved across the center. There were twenty seats in each row. Kate didn't know that, naturally, but as they began to take their seats, the boys hung back and the girls filled up the first row. Beverly Jean, grasping her two dearest friends in each hand, slid in to sit at about the middle of the row. Counting Kate, there were twenty-one girls in the class, so that by the time they had all jostled one another for a place in that first row, Kate found that if she was to sit with the class she would have to sit in the boys' row. Was that what was expected of her? She looked toward Beverly Jean, but that young lady was already happily engrossed in what was happening on the screen.

All at once Kate heard a whisper at her elbow.

"Here," said Vic. "I saw what was happening. I saved this seat next to me for you."

Kate looked down to see Vic seated on an aisle seat and in the gloom, she could see the vacant space next to him.

"Thanks," she whispered and slid across his knees into it.

The feature began finally and, after a very few minutes, Kate discovered to her utter surprise that she wasn't the least bit interested in it. You could tell to look at this little girl that no matter what happened, nothing would be permitted to muss up her hair. And whatever happened, everyone was going to end up by loving her and everyone connected with her even remotely was sure to live happily ever after. Suddenly Kate didn't care what happened to her. Her pouts, her bobbing curls were too nearly like Beverly Jean's for Kate's enjoyment.

"I'll bet she can be just as mean, too," she thought.

All at once she felt a cautious elbow pressing into her ribs.

"Do you like this?" Vic whispered.

"No," Kate whispered back.

"Let's beat it," Vic breathed into her ear.

Kate swung around to peer at him. Even in this murky light she could see that he was serious.

"We couldn't," she said. "We have to go to the party."

"O.K.," returned Vic. "We'll go to the party all right, but we don't have to sit here for two hours. Nobody'll miss us."

"Where'll we go?" asked Kate.

"Down to the wharf. Leo's there."

Kate began to do some rapid and sober thinking. To walk out on the picture was an appalling idea. She had never done such a thing in her life and to do so now when she was expected to sit patiently as a guest at a party was something Kate's rather unimaginative brain could never have pictured in its wildest flights. She thought of the wharf and compared with the shadowy antics being displayed before her, it had all the appeal of fresh air and sunshine to a victim smothering in a darkened pit. But what would happen if she went away? Kate's heart began to thump expectantly, because suddenly she knew that she was going. No matter what happened, to sit here any longer now, would be worse than anything that could happen to her.

"I'll go out first and wait for you," Vic was whispering. "It won't be so noticeable if we don't both go together."

Kate kept her eyes on the screen and felt rather than saw Vic leave. For a good three minutes, she waited, her heart pounding with what she was sure must be audible thumps. Then, swiftly, Kate slipped out of her seat. She gave one speeding glance down the row of seats to where Miss Morgan sat with Beverly Jean's mother and her friend. Then without a backward look, Kate walked as soundlessly as a mouse on velvet up the heavily carpeted incline toward the exit and freedom.

In the first blinding flash of light as she emerged onto the street, she saw Vic.

"Gosh," he greeted her, "I thought you'd changed your mind and weren't coming."

"What shall we do with the presents?" asked Kate, looking down at the dainty package Nora had wrapped for her.

"Put it in your pocket, the way I did mine," advised Vic.

"It'll crush," said Kate, feeling that it wouldn't be fair to Nora to spoil the looks of her handiwork.

"Leo will find a safe place for it," Vic assured her. "Come on."

They started up the street, but before they had gone ten paces, a voice came after them. "Kate," it called, "Kate Summers."

Kate stopped and slowly turned around. It was Miss Morgan.

"Don't you like the picture?" she asked.

"No," replied Kate.

"Where are you going?"

"To the wharf with Vic."

Miss Morgan looked at him then. "You two aren't being very polite," she informed them. "Running away from a party after you've arrived at it."

"We're coming to the party, Miss Morgan," Vic reassured her. "We just got tired of the movie."

"Yes," echoed Kate, adding, "and if we have to sit there we'll just wiggle and spoil it for the others."

"Yeah," agreed Vic, thinking that this was probably the

most brilliant idea Kate had ever had in the whole course of her life, "we sure would."

Miss Morgan looked at them for a moment, saying nothing, then, "Doesn't Mrs. Tuttle expect you to stay here at the theater?" she asked Kate.

"I'll phone her from somewhere and tell her," offered Kate.

"If you promise to do that," said Miss Morgan, "I'll let you go."

"I promise," said Kate.

"How about me?" demanded Vic.

Miss Morgan studied his anxious face for a moment, then smiled. "Might as well try to keep a fish away from water as a Corsatti," she said.

With that, they parted, Miss Morgan going back into the theater, and the two children starting off once more, and Kate, at least, much more happily, toward the wharf.

"Leo will tell you where you can phone," Vic told her.

"I'll do it first thing," answered Kate. And she did. Or almost the first thing.

Chapter VII

It's Sensible Sometimes

THE wharf ran far out into the blue bay. There were buildings out near the end and automobiles and pedestrians moved back and forth along the whole length of it. People were fishing along each side, sitting in the sun with their feet swinging over the edge and their poles reaching out patiently in front of them. Brilliant light danced over the lifting water on which floating gulls bobbed like feathered corks. Lifting and falling in the same rhythm, Kate saw the masts of the fishing fleet tied at one side near the end of the wharf. The boats were not yet visible, but as she and Vic quickened their steps, the masts lengthened and finally the hulls of the little craft bobbed in full view. They were of varying sizes, but none of them looked large enough for venturing upon such a wide ocean, Kate thought. Now the two came to where the fishing nets were spread to dry. Some were stretched along the edge of the wharf and men on up-ended boxes were mending them. Vic stopped beside one of them.

"Something make you a lot of trouble, Louie?" he asked.

The old man glanced up from his work, squinting at Vic through bushy gray eyebrows. His face was deeply tanned and deeply lined.

"Yeh, I have tough luck. Last night a baby sea lion he get all tangled up in my net and the mother she try to rescue him, so when I come home from fishing this morning, I have in my net one baby sea lion and many big holes. And no fish."

Louie shook his head sadly and returned to his net mending.

"What happened to the baby sea lion?" asked Vic. Kate leaned closer eagerly. This was exactly what she wanted to know.

"Oh, we bring him up and look at him a little bit and then I give him to one of the fellows. Later on, we kill him."

He shrugged, looked out across the water, and went on with his work. But now Kate broke into the conversation.

"No," she said quickly. "You mustn't kill him ever. Sea lions don't do any harm. We learned all about them in school. And besides, it's against the law to kill them."

Louie continued his mending in silence for a moment, then he laid his gnarled old hands on his knees and regarded her curiously, his head tipped to one side to avoid the direct sunlight.

"No-o-o-o?" he queried, and Kate felt her face grow red. "You talk much nonsense. A sea lion makes me lose one day's fishing. Without fish, I starve. And you say they do no harm. Maybe not you. That is true. But me they harm very much. And that is important to me. When it is necessary to decide which is important, Louie or the sea lion, I choose Louie every time. Even a sea lion can understand that."

Kate had stood there feeling small and ignorant as Louie had gone on talking. By the time he had finished she wished with all her heart that the planks of the wharf might close over her head, hiding her from public view. Louie was bent over his work again, seeming to have forgotten her entirely. He hadn't seemed angry. Not even bitter. Just very sure and decided about things.

You would have to be sure about things if your food depended on your decisions, she thought. She knew she would choose Kate every time, too. Louie was simply looking honestly and sensibly at things and she respected him for it. There was still, of course, the little matter of the law, but perhaps the people who made it hadn't understood Louie's side of it either. Anyway, it was the chance he'd have to take. Just like Cousin Ethel when she drove too fast.

Kate was glad, though, when Vic took leave of him and started on his way again. She was still feeling the scorn of his words and so her good-by to Louie's bowed shoulders was a timid murmur.

He didn't bother to look up. "Oh, I see you again lots of times," he said, and Kate thought it the nicest good-by she had ever heard. It made her feel a little closer to the ancient brotherhood of fishermen to have old Louie expect her to come back here "lots of times."

"There's Leo," cried Vic suddenly, throwing an excited look over his shoulder and breaking into a run.

Kate followed him blindly, wishing she possessed his knack of dodging cars, people, and coiled ropes as if they had not been there. All at once there was a shout, and Kate stopped so suddenly she almost lost her balance and went down.

"Hey, look where you're going. What do you think my nets are, a carpet for your feet, eh?"

Kate was standing where the shout had stopped her, right in the middle of a long length of orange-brown netting, and a young man, a tall young man, bronzed and handsome, with a head of black and crisply curling hair, was roaring right at her and grinning happily. His teeth were very white against his tanned skin. He couldn't be really angry and smile like that, she thought. But even as she watched him, the smile vanished, his brows drew together fiercely, and his dark eyes glared.

"Jump! Beat it, or I throw you into the ocean," he yelled, and started toward Kate.

Panic gave power to her legs. With a mighty leap, she cleared the nets, coming down onto the wharf planking with such force that the soles of her feet stung. There was a roar of laughter that might have been heard in China and Kate felt rage take complete possession of her whole being. So this was the wonderful Leo of whom Vic was so proud! This the big brother who was the best fisherman in the bay! This the Corsatti who was the best of the whole lot! Well, he was also the rudest. In fact, he was the rudest man she had ever known or ever hoped to know. The most impossible of all her loud-mouthed cousins seemed a gentleman when contrasted with this noisy and uncouth giant. Leo, indeed! She hated him. Even if she had walked on his nets, he needn't have frightened her to death. And then he had dared to laugh at her fright. She hated him!

"What are you fooling around here for?" Now he was

bullying Vic who was opening his mouth to reply. "Don't say a word," commanded Leo. "I know. You think maybe I take you and your girl friend for a ride, eh?"

He looked from Vic to Kate. "You pick a red head this time," he commented, "and she looks pretty mad. Red heads have bad tempers. Ain't that right, eh? Why do you look so mad?" He was grinning at Kate again.

This was really too much. Why, indeed! As if he didn't know. Would he never stop insulting her? She could feel tears stinging her eyes. Oh, why had she come out here with Vic in the first place? Why hadn't she done what was expected of her and stayed quietly at the movie? She turned her back on Leo and started blindly along the way she had come. She wanted to run, but the wharf was too wobbly through her tears. If only she could get away from this place she'd never come near it again. Never.

But Kate didn't get away. Not then, at least. A brown arm shot out and seized her, and a deeply contrite voice said from somewhere above her bent head, "Aw, now, you must not mind me." Leo's free hand took hold of her chin, and tilted her face back. "See, now, I am not really a bad guy. I just make a fool of myself sometimes. Vic is tough. All the kids I know, they're all tough. I forget maybe you are different. You must not cry, please."

Kate looked into his troubled face and deep into his dark eyes. She had never seen kinder eyes. And now they were troubled because she was troubled. She sniffed loudly, remembering she hadn't brought a handkerchief. Instantly,

Leo let go of her chin and fishing into a back pocket of his black jeans, handed her a flaming red bandanna.

"Here," he said, "it is perhaps fishy, but not too bad. Use it. I give it to you. A peace offering, eh?"

He held her at arm's length and looked eagerly, questioningly into her eyes. "Say we are friends."

Kate took the bandanna and wiped her eyes and nose. Vic had been wrong. Thank goodness, Leo *did* carry a handkerchief. "Sure," she said, "we're friends."

"O.K.," yelled Leo, giving her a slap on the shoulder that nearly knocked the wind out of her. "That's swell. Now all is made right again, and I take you for a ride."

With a bound, he was back at the wharf side, working with some ropes. "Come on, you kids," he called, and vanished below. "Let's go."

"Wait," cried Kate, suddenly remembering, "I have to phone Mrs. Tuttle."

Leo's head reappeared just above the wharf's edge so that it looked as if it had been lopped off his neck and carefully placed there.

"Over there," the head nodded miraculously toward a fish market on the other side of the wharf. "You can use theirs."

So Kate phoned Mrs. Tuttle who readily gave her permission to stay with Leo for the duration of the movie, but to be very careful of her dress for it was the best one she had. And when Kate left the fish market she no longer was carrying a dainty package wrapped in white tissue and tied with pink ribbon. It was lying safely on a clean piece of paper in the ice case alongside a tray of very raw and very fishy sand dabs. Kate was much relieved at the sight of it reposing there. It would probably smell a little fishy, she thought, but better that than to have Nora's white paper become soiled. Besides, she remembered sensibly, the cedar smell of the box itself would banish whatever strange odors might cling to its wrappings.

By the time she had returned to the wharf's edge where Leo had vanished, both he and Vic were standing in the boat tied to a float down below. Stairs led to the float, and it didn't take Kate very long to travel down them. In an instant, she was standing on the float with the sides of Leo's boat rubbing against it except when a swell rolled under them and lifted the boat a good two feet away. Kate started to wonder just how she would ever time her jump to land herself into the boat before the water drew it away again.

"Give me your hands," commanded Leo, reaching toward her. She laid her hands in his, and as his sinewy fingers closed over hers, she knew that as long as Leo was around, she had nothing to fear. He would get her safely into the boat.

"Jump," he yelled and, obeying blindly, Kate jumped, to feel herself lifted out over the water in a quick swing. The next thing she knew, there she was in the boat with Leo beside her. Vic was already seated in the stern sheets, as much at home as if he lived there.

Leo started the motor and with a steady put-put-put they began slowly to back away from the wharf. Kate lifted her eyes to the people fishing along its edge. They were all watching and it made her feel full of importance. She would have

been surprised to have known that several sitting idly there thought her red head made a pretty spot of color against the blue sea.

As soon as they were clear, Leo spun the wheel and the little craft headed into the open bay. This was Kate's very first boat ride, although she didn't say so. Vic and Leo were too much at home on the water for her to risk such a confession. It might draw their ridicule and just now she didn't want anything to spoil the perfection of this experience. Not even friendly ridicule.

"Can we go around the point to the lighthouse?" Vic shouted over the coughing of the motor.

Leo nodded and turned their course toward the stretch of land reaching like a long arm into the bay. It was fun to be so close to the water without being actually in it, Kate thought, watching the soapy bubbles that floated in their wake. The farther they got from the wharf, the more the bow plunged up and down. Once, when a swell lifted them and let them fall back into its trough, there was such a heavy plop that spray was flung like rain into their faces.

"Hey, whatcha trying to do?" yelled Vic.

But Leo only laughed and said, "We baptize Kate with salt water. Now she is a real sailor."

Kate, watching the water roll away from them in great oily swells, wondered what a storm at sea would be like. Surely no boat as tiny as this could last long in a storm. After only a little hesitation, she asked Leo about it.

"Sure I get caught in storms, but a storm is as nothing to my *Lena*. This is my girl friend," patting the boat, "and she

III

is always true to me." Leo threw back his head and laughed mightily. *"Lena* and I, we don't worry about storms, we don't worry about nothing so long as the fish run, eh Vic?"

He looked around to discover that Vic had a line over the side and was hanging half-way into the water to watch it.

Instantly, Leo's face became wild and excited. "Are you crazy?" he yelled. "You can't trawl at this speed. We go too fast."

"I know," said Vic, pulling himself back into the boat and grinning sheepishly at Leo. "But I just like to play I'll get one."

Leo flung up his hands and his handsome face beamed.

"There is a true fisherman," he said to Kate. "No Corsatti but would fish in a bucket if he had nothing better. Wherever there is water, they must have a line in it. Always fishermen. Always poor. Always happy."

He flashed Kate his white smile then left her to her own thoughts. At that moment she would rather have been a fisherman than anything else in the world. Leo was proud that all his family had been and would continue to be fishermen. Good fishermen. Even though they never got rich, he was still proud. And happy. Rising and falling and always plowing steadily forward through green water, Kate remembered suddenly what Nora had said that day they had cleaned house together and Kate had asked her what was more important than making money. What was it Nora had said? Slowly the words came back to Kate as from a great distance.

"Being happy, having the courage of your own convictions, and being independent."

Somehow they all seemed tied up together; you couldn't have the first without the other two. Leo seemed to have acquired all three, as had Christopher. And, like Christopher, he was one of the pleasantest people she knew, as well as the happiest. Could there be something, after all, in what Nora had said?

Off Lighthouse Point they saw a few sea lions gliding through the water as if they were water themselves. Kate had never seen anything so effortless as the ease of their swimming. Leo stopped the motor and the three sat quietly and watched them. Now there was no sound but the water slapping the boat's sides. Once in a while one of the sea lions would blow the water from his nostrils with a snort that sounded unnaturally loud.

"Louie found a baby one in his net this morning," Kate said, very quietly.

"Old Louie had a pipe dream," returned Leo. "This is a little early for baby sea lions."

"Yeh, Leo, he said he saw it." Vic came scrambling over from the stern to verify Kate's words.

"I know," said Leo, nodding, his narrowed eyes on the rocks where two sea lions lay sunning themselves. "But it is funny."

"You won't kill it, will you?" asked Kate.

"Sea lions are bad business," replied Leo.

"But this is just a baby," argued Kate.

"Babies grow up," affirmed Leo.

"Where is it now?" asked Vic.

"It is here," said Leo, and reaching forward drew from un-

113

der the bow sheets a gunny sack tied with rope at one end.

"You had it all the time?" demanded Kate, too astonished to speak sensibly. Obviously, Leo must have had it all the time.

"Sure. I took it away from old Louie to show it to Vic. Anyway, that's what I let him think. He was going to kill it and I sure don't blame him any. But me, I get all soft inside when I see it. It's too little. I cannot bear to hurt little things. I guess I got no sense."

"Oh, yes," Kate was saying inside herself, as she watched Leo cutting the rope, "you've got more sense than anyone I know."

Carefully, Leo rolled back the sack to reveal a little snout from which stiff whiskers bristled up. Followed bulging eyes and a fat little body covered with fur so fine and sleek it looked like skin instead of fur. It struggled under Leo's hands, its flippers trying to brace themselves against the thwarts, but he held it firmly while the two children bent over to look closely at it. Kate thought it the most lovable thing she had ever seen and longed to take it in her arms and hug it. It looked so like a baby and so little and helpless, she quite understood how even a fisherman like Leo could take pity on it. But, then, Louie had wanted to kill it and he, too, was a fisherman. She was suddenly terribly glad that Leo possessed more heart than good sense.

"I guess we're close enough in now," said Leo at last, measuring the distance to shore. Kate noticed that they had drifted quite close to the point. "Look out, you kids, I'm going to put him over the side."

Carefully, Leo's great brown hands circled the soft body and more quickly than Kate's eyes could follow him, lifted the baby sea lion into the sea. Instantly it dove, reappearing a few seconds later at a safe distance from the boat.

"I hope its old lady is among that crowd over there," he said. "I got a good hunch she is."

Kate looked at him. No wonder Vic spoke with such pride of this big brother. He had planned all along to bring the little sea lion out here. He had just waited for them to go along, too. Leo was kind. He was kind and good. She liked him. With all her heart, she liked him.

After that, they put about and started back toward the wharf. Just before they got there, Leo cut the motor and the boat's momentum carried them gently up to the float.

"Hey, you kids," Leo called them to him as they were making ready to jump to the float. "Don't say anything about the sea lion up there," jerking his chin toward the row of feet over their heads. "They'd think I was one first-class sap."

"No," promised Kate and Vic together. "We won't."

Climbing back up the flight of steps to the wharf's edge, Kate thought how nice it was to have two secrets with two of her favorite grown-ups all in the space of one week. And then another thought came to her and so surprised her that she let Leo get away without thanking him for her good time. Neither one of these grown-ups really had good sense!

When Kate caught sight of Christopher coming toward her along the wharf a few minutes later, she had the distinct feeling that something had happened. Something important. His first words gave no hint of it, however.

"Thought you were at a party," he said.

"We were. We are. That is, we're going to be," said Kate in some confusion.

"Suppose you take time out and sort your answers," said Christopher.

"Well, Vic and I got tired of the movie, but we're going back to give our presents and have refreshments," explained Kate.

"But weren't you expected to stay at the movie?" he asked.

Kate nodded, suddenly a little worried. Then Christopher said a most surprising thing. He said, "How do you like changing the pattern, Kate?"

Her eyes were questioning as they stared into his.

"Don't you remember the other day out on the cliff when I asked you why you didn't change the pattern sometime and you said you'd better stick to being sensible and do what was expected of you?"

Kate grinned and nodded. "I guess sometimes it's sensible to change the pattern," she said.

"And if ever it agreed with anyone, it does with you," Christopher replied. "I haven't seen you look so happy, Kate."

Kate didn't know what to reply to this, so she very sensibly kept still.

For another moment, Christopher stood looking at her. At last he said, "I've just come to a momentous decision. Something rather important has happened. May I come over to your house this evening to discuss it with you, Kate? I'd like Mr. and Mrs. Tuttle's opinion, too."

"Sure," answered Kate, too surprised to be more gracious. "Will Nora come too?"

"I doubt it," said Christopher. "Nora's getting to be a regular old stick-in-the-mud. Doesn't seem to want to go anywhere."

Kate looked sharply at him and there was amusement as well as wisdom in the gray depths of her eyes. Evidently Nora hadn't told him a word about the secret. She was glad.

"Then I'll see you sometime after supper," he said, moving away. "You and Vic had better hustle back to that movie if you want to go over to Beverly Jean's house with the rest of the crowd."

Vic and Kate rejoined their classmates just as the group was filing out of the theater. No one except, of course, Miss Morgan, seemed to have noticed their absence. Mrs. Brown, her friend, and Miss Morgan got into the new Buick with white-walled tires and drove off, while Beverly Jean graciously walked home with her guests.

The house to which she took them was exactly like advertisements in magazines, Kate decided. Everyone was considerably awed by its elegance and found it difficult to talk when first ushered into the spacious living-room. Kate noticed that it was spotless and wondered, professionally, how many people it would take to keep such a large house in such faultless condition. Then Beverly Jean's mother, together with Miss Morgan, started some games and everyone had a very good time.

Kate was a little disappointed that they didn't have their

refreshments in the dining-room. She heard Beverly Jean's mother say something in an aside to Miss Morgan about "all these children and my new rug." But, Kate thought with inner satisfaction, it wouldn't have held them all anyway. There couldn't be a dining-room in the world large enough to hold forty people. However, the ice cream and birthday cake tasted very good out on the sun porch. A long table had been rigged on saw horses down the whole length of the glassed-in porch which stretched along one side of the house and here Beverly Jean held court with as much grace as any princess. It was like a movie to watch her, Kate thought.

The presents had been surrendered on arrival, and were now heaped in a rather considerable pyramid at Beverly Jean's place. Animatedly, she began opening them. As Vic had predicted, most of them were handkerchiefs, so that when Kate's lone pencil box came to view, it was accorded a very flattering welcome. If there was any fishy smell clinging to it, Beverly Jean didn't let on. She lifted the lid, took a deep whiff of the cedar smell, admired the picture on the cover, and declared it "perfect."

"Nora Cline made it, and Christopher did the picture," Kate said, determined that Beverly Jean should know at once that it was home-made and repudiate it forthwith if she so wished.

But, "Really?" cried Beverly Jean. Then, jerking toward her mother who was hovering at her side, "Look, Mummie," she said, "a pencil box, and every bit of it hand-made!"

Kate wondered if there could be a difference between pencil boxes and valentines. Or did the difference lie in who happened to be on the receiving end, Beverly Jean or somebody else? But she *was* pretty sitting there unwrapping presents, reading cards, and thanking one and all.

Later, Beverly Jean did a tap dance for them and then the children were allowed to depart. As she and Vic trudged home together, Kate wondered how she would manage to last until that vague time known as "after supper" when she could expect Christopher to divulge his "momentous decision."

Chapter VIII

A Portrait and a Problem

IT WAS quiet in the Tuttle living-room except for the rattle of pages as Kate leafed through the magazines she was sorting. Now and then, Mr. Tuttle read aloud a paragraph from the article he was reading to Mrs. Tuttle who was busy with her mending. Kate didn't listen carefully because this evening she was occupied with comparing the advertisements with Beverly Jean's house. Besides, the article didn't seem to have anything good to say of the state of the world and Kate had had too good a time today to be in a proper mood for such sober discussion. And the best part was yet to come. Every footfall on the street outside brought her head up into an alert and listening position. It might be Christopher.

It was almost Kate's bedtime when at last he did appear. As he greeted the Tuttles, she watched him closely and decided that he looked just like a person who had something very important to tell. After only a brief discussion with Mr. Tuttle about the article he had been reading on the desperate state of the world, Christopher began explaining the reason for his visit.

"You probably are familiar with *The Woman's Housekeeping Journal*," he said to Mrs. Tuttle.

"Oh my, yes," she replied. "I've taken it for years. Kate's been sorting magazines this evening. There must be a dozen *Journals* there. Aren't there, Kate?"

Kate was about to start counting, when Christopher stopped her.

"It's all right," he said. "I just wanted to be sure you knew it. You see, they've opened a contest to artists for the selection of a series of cover drawings. I'm going to enter the contest and I'd like to borrow Kate if you don't mind."

"Me?" cried Kate, wondering what on earth she could have to do with *The Woman's Housekeeping Journal*'s contest.

"Yes," said Christopher, hitching forward on his chair. His face was shining with enthusiasm. "I decided today at the wharf," looking directly at Kate, "that I wanted you for my model. I think I've wanted you ever since the other morning when I first saw you out on the cliff. I want to pose you with the whole wide ocean at your back and with that look of serene balance and confident gladness that you had on your face today. And I want to call the picture 'Sensible Kate.'"

It was a thundering announcement and it left Kate stunned and bewildered. She, an artist's model! She, red-haired and freckled with never a dimple anywhere! It was unthinkable. Perhaps Christopher was making fun of her. She stole a quick look at him and dropped her eyes back to her lap, ashamed. No, Christopher would never make fun of anybody. Not

Christopher. He must actually want her to pose for him. But it was the strangest thing she'd ever heard of.

"Well, what do you say?" Christopher's voice sliced loudly across the silence that had wrapped itself around his astounding speech.

Kate answered with the words that were already drumming in her brain. "I'm not pretty," she said.

"That's why I want you," explained Christopher with somewhat brutal frankness. "I don't want this to be just a pretty child picture. I want it to say something. Your face has things in it, Kate, and it's adding more things every day. That's why I want to borrow it."

Kate shrugged in sudden awkward shyness. "It's all right with me," she said, as if such offers were made to her every day.

Then Christopher took up the discussion with the Tuttles. They talked for several minutes back and forth, but Kate never heard a word of what was said. All she could hear was a little voice deep inside of her which kept repeating, "He wants to call it *Sensible Kate!* He wants to call it *Sensible Kate!*"

It was planned that Kate should pose for Christopher on Saturdays and Sundays and after school. With spring vacation just a few weeks away, the matter of Kate's free time presented little difficulty. But when Christopher became businesslike and mentioned the matter of model's fees, Kate took a decided stand.

"I won't take any money," she said. "It'll be fun doing it. I can be with you and Nora most of the time. And besides," she added, with characteristic practicalness, "you don't know whether you're going to be paid for it ever, or not."

Christopher laughed, reaching out to draw her close to him.

"Have it your way," he said, "but there'll be a settlement later, young lady," he added darkly.

So, in one short week, there began for Kate a whole new existence. Things happen quickly when one is ten years old. The reason is simple. When you are that age, you make things happen. Later, as a grown-up, you are content merely to wait for things to happen. Waiting always makes time move slowly. If you are sensible it is possible when you are ten, to make a week worth a month of any grown-up's life, while a month is as good as a year ten years later. Kate felt quite positive that no week in all the rest of her life would be as full of meaning and of change as this one. And she was quite right in feeling so.

On the surface, the change was not so great. She still helped Mrs. Tuttle with the housework, she still played with Vic, she still went to school. But for the first time in her life, she had a chance to sit quietly without feeling guilty about it. And when you sit quietly, you have a chance to think and to sort your thoughts. Sitting, sometimes outdoors, sometimes in, Kate had ample opportunity to consider the matter of being cute as compared with the matter of being sensible. The more she thought about it, the more necessary it seemed that she change her previous notions with respect to both. For there was no arguing the fact that had she been merely pretty like Beverly Jean, Christopher would never have asked her to pose for his picture.

He had said as much. And the picture meant a great deal to him. It was no practice sketch. It was of tremendous importance. On it depended in large measure the establishment of Christopher's success as an artist. With it, he might be able to justify his refusal to go to work in his father's office. And he was staking all this on Kate's own face. Because, as he had said, there were things in it.

Was being sensible as desirous, after all, as being pretty? Kate asked herself this question many times. And always she followed it with an answer that was doubtless very sensible, though it may not have been very wise. It would all depend, she warned herself, on whether or not Christopher's "Sensible Kate" won the contest. The verdict would surely be reached then.

Sometimes while Kate sat for Christopher, Nora would read aloud stories which a few weeks ago would have seemed to Kate silly but which, now that her horizons had widened to the far-flung limits of the sea, seemed not only logical, but enjoyable. They were for the most part written by that same Hans Christian Andersen whose story of the darning needle Nora had told her on the first day of their acquaintance. Kate's favorite of all these stories, because she understood it best, Christopher banned during work hours. He said it made her eyes a little too sober as she listened to it. That story was "The Ugly Duckling."

Those were lovely, tranquil stretches of time during which Kate sat with her back to the sea, hearing the rush of breakers behind her as an accompaniment to Nora's voice. In front of her, the hills lifted gentle green slopes up from the town.

Some days they were spotted with cloud shadows while farther out cloud banks circled the whole horizon, rising up from the farthest rim of the sea. In shallow canyons, a few late-blooming acacias flaunted their bright yellow, their color a gay defiance to the dark line of pines soberly holding the hill top. It was spring now, and though still too early for the tourist season, each day brought more and more people to the beach.

One morning during spring vacation, Kate noticed an old woman standing on the very top of a pile of rocks which rose straight up from the water's edge. She had a bucket to which was fastened a long rope and she was lowering the bucket on the rope over the side of the rocks into the water. Kate was too far away to see her face, but instantly she remembered the old woman in the house next door to the Tuttles whom she had seen one day with just such a bucket in her hand. The old woman, Kate had found out, was Mrs. Withers and in accordance with her own expressed wish, Kate, beyond discovering her name, had let her strictly alone. Now, as on that other occasion, she was curious about her. Though she had learned the purpose of the rope and the bucket, she still felt as if she must know why Mrs. Withers required sea water. When Christopher declared a rest period, Kate began sauntering down the beach in the direction of the rock pile.

When she had got almost up to it, Kate paused to watch Mrs. Withers' strange behavior. She was hauling up the bucket filled with water, scrutinizing its contents carefully, and dumping the water back into the surf again. She did this three times before Kate, remembering vividly that this weird old woman didn't like children, overcame her fears enough to call out, "What are you doing?"

Slowly, Mrs. Withers swung around on her perch atop the rock and looked down at Kate.

"Curiosity killed a cat," she said.

Kate pondered this in silence while Mrs. Withers filled and dumped another bucket.

At last she called up. "But curiosity might save a cat's life."

The old woman looked down at her again. "There's sense in that," she admitted. Then, "I'm getting sea water as anyone should be able to see for himself."

"Oh, I know that," Kate said pleasantly, "but what are you trying to get besides?"

"Just water," came the reply briefly.

"But you must have water at home," argued Kate, rather amused at Mrs. Withers' queerness. "All you have to do is turn on the faucet and there it is."

Mrs. Withers threw her bucket back into the water, then turned toward Kate and said slowly and emphatically, "You can't get the Pacific Ocean by turning on a faucet."

Kate weighed this remark while again Mrs. Withers pulled the rope up, hand over hand. Kate could hear the bucket scraping against the sides of the rock in its ascent. Now what had this funny old woman meant by that? It stood to reason that you couldn't get the Pacific Ocean by turning on a faucet. The remark had the ring of a proverb like, "seconds are the gold dust of time," or something like that. What had Mrs. Withers meant? Kate never left herself in doubt about things

126

long. She had always found the direct method the best approach to any problem. So now she called up to the top of the rock, "What did you mean by what you just said?"

Mrs. Withers peered down at her again. "Well, can you?" she asked.

"No, of course you can't," said Kate thoughtfully. The idea of turning on a faucet and getting the Pacific Ocean!

"And you'll find it true all your life," prophesied Mrs. Withers.

"Find what true?" asked Kate.

"That the bigger and more important things are, the harder they are to come by."

Like being wise and beautiful, thought Kate, and understood perfectly.

Mrs. Withers had got a bucket of water that apparently satisfied her and now she was coming cautiously down the rock pile with it.

"What do you do with the water?" Kate asked, when she had reached the sand.

Mrs. Withers hesitated a moment, studying Kate with open dislike. "You ask more questions than most young ones. No manners at all. None." She started away, then stopped and looked around at Kate. "I soak my feet in it," she added.

Kate wanted to laugh, but there was that about Mrs. Withers that made laughter in her presence seem out of place. But Kate no longer felt afraid of her. It is impossible to fear anyone who soaks her feet in a bucket of sea water. And with the disappearance of that former fear, Kate's daring rose proportionately within her. There was one more question she felt she had to have answered. It had gnawed at her off and on ever since that first morning at the Tuttles when she had tried to pilfer a few violets from around Mrs. Withers' cypress.

"Why don't you like children?" she asked.

Mrs. Withers continued to plod through the sand, trying to spill as little water out of her bucket as possible. Kate trotted forward to walk beside her.

"Children have no manners nowadays," said Mrs. Withers. "They have only self-expression."

"All children?" queried Kate.

"All," echoed the old woman. "Especially you."

Kate rather resented this. Her manners might not be perfect she was quite willing to admit, but they weren't as bad as Mrs. Withers would have her believe.

"I don't think my manners are any worse than yours," she defended herself. "And I'm a lot more sensible."

"That is strictly a matter of opinion. If you had really good sense you'd go about your affairs and leave me to mine."

"And someday," added Kate, more to herself than to the person beside her, "someday I'm going to be wise."

Christopher had said that sometimes wise people are beautiful.

"That's good news," said Mrs. Withers and chuckled. "And if you are going to continue living next door to me, it may even prove stimulating," she continued.

"Why?" asked Kate.

"A wise enemy is of more value to you than a foolish friend. Keeps you on your toes."

They had reached the street, and Kate knew she must return to Christopher and the portrait.

"But I don't want to be your enemy," said Kate. "Isn't there anything I could do to make you like me?"

Mrs. Withers set down her bucket and looked at Kate with eyes as hostile as they had ever been. "Yes," she said, "there is just one thing you can do."

Kate's face brightened, "What?"

"You can spend the next ten years quietly growing," was Mrs. Withers' reply. "I can even find myself looking forward to the time when you are grown-up. Especially, if you continue to live next door to me," she added, picking up her bucket and leaving Kate standing speechless on the curb.

Kate looked after her, a frown deepening between her eyes. Mrs. Withers had said things that were full of meaning but which sounded queer! Did wise people talk this way? Was Mrs. Withers wise? It was a disturbing thought, because Christopher had once told her that wisdom and beauty sometimes went hand in hand. Certainly, Mrs. Withers was no beauty. Did she, Kate, run the risk of acquiring wisdom only to look like Mrs. Withers? Would she end up by disliking children, too? Suddenly, Kate knew that Mrs. Withers wasn't wise. There was no more wisdom in her disliking all children than in her, Kate's, suddenly deciding that she disliked all old women. It didn't make sense. And people who didn't make sense, just couldn't be wise. That didn't make sense, either.

It was during spring vacation, too, that Miss Watson from the county office called to see Kate. She had been out to call on Mrs. Tuttle twice before, but Kate had always been in school and so had missed her. It was afternoon when she came. The luncheon dishes had been washed, and Kate, idly watching Mrs. Tuttle ironing window curtains, was thinking of going over to Lighthouse Avenue, when the doorbell jangled.

"Oh, rats," said Mrs. Tuttle, who was right in the middle of a curtain length. "Probably an agent. Go to the door, Kate, and tell whoever's there that we don't want anything."

Kate went to the door and found Miss Watson on the other side of it. "Hello," she said. "How nice to find you home. I've come to take you for a ride if Mrs. Tuttle is willing."

"Come in," said Kate. "I'll go see."

She showed Miss Watson into the living-room and returned to the kitchen. Mrs. Tuttle looked up from wriggling the iron into six inches of ruffle. "Who was it?" she asked.

"It's Miss Watson from the county office and she's come to take me riding with her if you'll let me go."

"Oh," said Mrs. Tuttle, yanking the electric cord out of the flatiron and whipping off her apron in almost one movement.

"I can finish the curtain while you talk to her," offered Kate.

Mrs. Tuttle looked at her sharply for a second. "Well, all right," she said reluctantly, "if you think you can."

"I've done it before," said Kate and connected the iron again.

Mrs. Tuttle gave her faultlessly neat hair a pat and hustled into the living-room.

Kate finishing up the ruffle could just barely hear the low voices of the two women as they talked. She knew they were talking about her and she wasn't the least bit worried. You don't need to worry when you have tried to do just what was expected of you. Not one little cloud was drifting on Kate's horizon as she reviewed her weeks with the Tuttles. She had broken a few dishes, true enough, but they had been accidents and she was sure Mrs. Tuttle hadn't held them against her. And sometimes she hadn't been on hand when Mrs. Tuttle had wanted her. But anyone is entitled to make a few mistakes. On the whole, she had been a good and sensible child and so there was nothing to worry about. And she was certain of Mrs. Tuttle's friendship. Sliding a width of curtain over the board to attack a new section of it, Kate felt quite satisfied with herself.

And then, right smack in the midst of her nice safe feeling, a new idea hit her and so stunned her that she almost scorched the curtain. Suppose Miss Watson had come to take her away? She had said they were going riding, and that could mean anything. It might just be an easy way of breaking the news to her that she was going to a new place. It didn't really matter to the county where she lived as long as she was safe and well. Perhaps the county had made a new decision about her. Perhaps Cousin Ethel wanted her back! And there was the picture to finish! And everything else, besides! Suddenly Kate knew real panic. She didn't stop to think. She didn't remember to act sensibly at all. She didn't even stop to remember that you always disconnect a flatiron before you leave it for any length of time. She hesitated just long enough to up-end it, thus saving the curtain, before she dashed from the kitchen into the presence of two very surprised women.

"I don't want to go away," she shouted, although she was standing squarely in front of Miss Watson. "And I won't go back to Cousin Ethel. If you make me, I'll be a problem. I promise. I won't do one thing right. Not one."

Miss Watson let her shout herself out, then said in exaggeratedly calm tones, "My word, that *was* an outburst. And children who say 'I won't' are already problems. I'm surprised, Kate, that you should become one. You've always seemed such a sensible child. What has come over you?"

Kate could feel the tension oozing out of her like a balloon going flat. As her excitement died down, her brain went to work again, and no sooner had this happened, than she realized she had jumped to conclusions. She should have asked first what they intended doing with her. She would ask now.

"Are you going to take me away?"

"No," said Miss Watson. "Mrs. Tuttle has been very happy to have you here and she wants you to stay. And since you have made it fairly plain that you want to, why, that takes care of that."

Kate stopped following the crazy pattern of Mrs. Tuttle's living-room rug to look at Miss Watson. She was smiling in that aren't-you-ashamed-of-yourself way that grown-ups have. But Kate wasn't ashamed. She was too glad to feel anything except gladness. Then, without even looking at Mrs. Tuttle whose pleased expression might have been a comfort to her at that moment, Kate turned without a word and went back to her ironing.

She had not quite finished with the curtain when Mrs. Tuttle came into the kitchen. "Miss Watson is waiting for you," she said, taking the iron from Kate. Then, rather timidly, she slid an arm around the little girl. "I'm glad you feel the way you do, and I'm going to tell Mr. Tuttle, too. We've both grown very fond of you, Kate."

Kate tried very hard to think of something to say, but couldn't. Affection was something she had experienced so rarely in her life that she was wholly unprepared to deal with it now. Besides, the chief reason she wanted to remain with the Tuttles was on account of Nora and Christopher whom she loved more than any other people she had ever known or ever would know, she felt sure.

As much as she liked the Tuttles, it was not wholly on their account that she had flown out at Miss Watson, although Mrs. Tuttle obviously took it that way. Should she, in her usual forthright manner, tell the truth? Or would it be better to leave Mrs. Tuttle in ignorance of the Clines' place in her affections and just let her go on thinking as she did?

Something told Kate it would hurt Mrs. Tuttle to know the whole truth. And something also told her it was unwise to hurt people unless it was unavoidable. She wouldn't tell, she decided at last, standing within the circle of Mrs. Tuttle's arm and hoping she wouldn't misunderstand her silence. And with that decision, Kate took her first step on the long road to wisdom. For the first time in her life, she had let her heart do the deciding.

A few minutes later, as Kate got into Miss Watson's car, Miss Watson said, "Where shall we go first? This is your afternoon, and I'm just going to take orders."

"Let's follow along the cliff and then go down to the beach," said Kate promptly.

"Good," said Miss Watson. "I'm so glad you didn't just say 'I don't care.'"

As they drove along the cliff road which wound in and out in deference to the sea's inroads upon the land, Kate told Miss Watson about her weeks with the Tuttles, about Vic and Beverly Jean, about her ride in Leo's boat (not mentioning, of course, the baby sea lion) and about Christopher and Nora and *The Woman's Housekeeping Journal* contest. Even about the house next door with cactus planted in the violet bed.

At last Kate was completely talked out, so Miss Watson who had been quietly listening all this time, took over the conversation.

"The Tuttles seem to have grown very fond of you, Kate," she said.

Kate didn't answer. There's nothing you can say to a statement like that except, "I'm glad," and certainly Miss Watson knew she would feel that way so there was no use saying it.

"I shouldn't be at all surprised if they might want you to stay with them always. Would you like that, Kate?"

"You mean they want to adopt me?" asked Kate.

"Well," said Miss Watson slowly, "they might want to."

So it had happened at last. Somebody wanted to adopt her! The decision she had been dreading most of her life had now presented itself. How did she feel about it? What did she want? The Tuttles had been good to her. But they were old. It was hard for them to remember how children felt about things. Mrs. Tuttle, especially, although she tried hard to remember.

That was just the trouble, Kate decided, she tried too hard. It made you conscious all the time that you really didn't belong to them nor they to you. She could never feel easy around them the way one should feel around one's own people. She felt closer to Mr. Tuttle, but he was away most of the time and still remained something of a stranger.

Still, if the Tuttles did adopt her, she wouldn't have to worry about being sent back to Cousin Ethel. And she wouldn't ever have to leave Christopher and Nora. She knew this was the hub of the whole problem. She could never endure separation from the Clines.

And then an appalling idea came to unsettle her mind just when she was on the point of telling Miss Watson that she wouldn't mind having the Tuttles adopt her after all. Suppose Christopher and Nora should leave this town! Suppose they did and she were the Tuttles' little girl! What would she do then? What could she do, if she belonged to the Tuttles? It would be terrible. Somehow, there was comfort in being free. The minute you belonged to anyone, that settled everything. No, she didn't want to be adopted. Not yet at least. Not until she was sure that everything was going to stay the way it was.

"Do I have to decide right away?" she asked Miss Watson.

"Oh, no, in fact I think it would be better if you thought it over for a while."

"That's what I'll do," said Kate thankfully. "I'll think it over real hard."

The road brought them down to the beach at last and to the hot-dog stand where Miss Watson bought two hot dogs. They ate them sitting on the very rocks where Mrs. Withers had hauled up the sea water.

When they had finished they built a sand castle and then Miss Watson and Kate drove back along the cliff road on a roundabout way home. The sun was going down and the sea and sky were tinged a deep pink. Everything seemed touched with the same soft glow except three gulls winging over the water and they were like shadow gulls, as dark as black velvet. For just a few moments, the strange light lingered, and then in an instant the world was gray and the gulls had taken back their own silver.

Chapter IX

Ocean-Going

THAT very same evening, Mr. Tuttle said with his eye on Mrs. Tuttle, "I've been thinking we need a dog."

"You are quite right, Andrew," said Mrs. Tuttle, not looking up from her sewing. "For thirty years of our married life, we have been able to manage quite nicely without one. But now we need a dog."

"I was thinking of Kate," said Mr. Tuttle.

"So was I," returned his wife.

Kate, busy with some spool knitting which she hoped in time would result in a rug for her room, said, "What kind of dog?"

"I haven't made up my mind," returned Mr. Tuttle. "But a friend of mine in the furniture business gets mattress samples. Real little mattresses with inner springs and everything, and one of them would make a fine bed for a dog. I thought we might get a dog to fit one of those mattresses."

"That's very sensible," said Kate, "and we could pick out a harness just about the size of a dog to fit the mattress, and then when we found the dog, we could just put the harness on him and lead him away."

"You two are the limit. Getting a dog to fit a harness to fit a mattress! I never heard of such a business," said Mrs. Tuttle.

"It's an excellent plan and saves a lot of speculation and argument," said Mr. Tuttle. "What would you like to name him?" he asked Kate.

Kate thought for several moments and then replied, "I think 'Skipper' would be a good name for an ocean-going dog."

That was a term she had learned after frequent visits to the wharf. There it seemed to matter a great deal whether a boat was "ocean-going" or not. Since only the best ones were, it had come to mean a mark of special merit to Kate. Naturally, her dog would be of the best. Therefore, ocean-going. She explained this to the Tuttles who accepted it without comment.

" 'Skipper' seems a good name to me," Mr. Tuttle said. "It's short and would fit a smallish dog. Sunday we'll call at the pound and see what they have there."

"May I put the little mattress beside my bed when we get it?" Kate asked Mrs. Tuttle.

Mrs. Tuttle looked up at her, concern in her face. "You mean you want the dog to sleep in your room?" she asked.

Kate nodded, wishing for one traitorous moment that Mrs. Tuttle was just a little bit like Cousin Ethel. Cousin Ethel wouldn't have minded.

"Has it seemed lonesome sleeping upstairs, Kate?" Mrs. Tuttle still looked concerned. "I never stopped to think you might have been afraid to sleep off there by yourself."

"Oh, no," said Kate quickly. "I like having my own room.

It was the first thing I liked about this place. But it would be nice to have my own dog there."

"Since it's your room, and you take all the care of it, I don't suppose I have any reason to object," said Mrs. Tuttle. "But, understand, I won't have him in any other part of the house. Not even for a minute. And you'll have to bring him in through the front door. I won't have him in my kitchen."

"Yes," replied Kate. "I'll remember."

Later, after she had gone to bed but before she had dropped off to sleep, Kate heard Mrs. Tuttle come to the foot of the stairs and stop there. She listened, expecting her to call up to her. But Mrs. Tuttle just stood there as if she were waiting. Kate lay perfectly still, waiting, too. Was she by any chance going to come up? She held her breath and her heart gave a little jump under her flannelette nightgown. It had never happened before. No one had ever tucked her into bed. At least not for as long as she could remember. How should she act? What should she say? It would probably seem funny to Mrs. Tuttle, too, not ever having had any children to tuck in until now. Then, while she waited, she heard Mrs. Tuttle go on into her own room and shut the door. She wasn't coming up after all!

Kate slowly relaxed while a let-down feeling flooded her. Now that Mrs. Tuttle wasn't coming up, she knew she had wanted her to, most awfully. A lump of lonesomeness began swelling in her throat, but she promptly swallowed it. What had come over her, anyway? Mrs. Tuttle had said good-night, and that was all anyone not a baby should expect her to do or even wish her to do. It was silly for a ten-year-old girl to want to be tucked into bed. Why, she was behaving like Cousin Ethel's youngest, only worse, for there was some excuse for a baby's acting so.

Kate pulled the covers close under her chin. She shut her eyes tight and heard the ocean whispering along the beach. She listened to it, thinking that it must be running up the sand now and around the rocks where she and Miss Watson had eaten their hot dogs. Perhaps at this very instant it was melting the sand castle they had built together. Suddenly, she wasn't one bit lonesome. The sound of the ocean was as friendly as a kitten's purring or a dog's contented breathing. Soon she was going to have a dog of her own, and Mrs. Tuttle had said it could sleep in her room. She'd tuck it into its little bed every night. And, thinking of that bed, Kate smiled into the dark and smiling, fell asleep. Like a really sensible child.

The very next Sunday, Kate and Mr. Tuttle went down to the corner drug store and bought a dog harness and a leash. Mrs. Tuttle had voiced objections when she found out what they were setting out for. But, "the better the day, the better the dog," Mr. Tuttle had calmly told her without pausing in his stride through the front hall, and Kate had followed right along in his wake. For a meek man, Mr. Tuttle could be very authoritative at times.

With the harness and leash, the two set out by bus for the pound where ownerless dogs were kept for a time until their owners should call for them. After the time was up, anyone could have his pick of the dogs not claimed upon payment of five dollars.

But disappointment greeted them there. Though there seemed to be a sufficiently representative mixture of dogs inside the several pens to have formed a canine League of Nations, only one miserable and mangy specimen would fit the harness. That is, only one of those available. There were many attractive and heartily friendly yappers standing on hind legs behind the wire fences, but these were all waiting to be called for. Only the most hopeless-looking curs could legally go home with Kate and she didn't want any of them curled at the side of her bed. None of them looked ocean-going.

As they stood waiting for the return bus and Kate was trying without success to convince herself that since she had never had a dog it didn't greatly matter if she never did have one, Mr. Tuttle said, "There's a place on the way into town that has Boston puppies for sale. I saw the sign on the way out here. We have five dollars to invest in a dog. Bostons are common now. I think we can get a puppy for that."

Kate gasped. A Boston puppy! A little fat, sleek, cuddly thing as near like a baby seal as anything in dogdom could be! Then she remembered the harness.

"It wouldn't fit the harness," she said.

"It would in about six months, or even a little less. And in the meantime, we could get a smaller harness."

That hurdle was safely crossed, but another and higher one loomed.

"Mrs. Tuttle wouldn't want it in the house and a little puppy couldn't live outside." Kate was sure Mr. Tuttle would never dare risk his wife's good nature up to this point.

"We could buy it with the privilege of returning it if she

objected too strenuously. But Mrs. Tuttle is never hard on young things. And puppies can be very appealing."

Mr. Tuttle made it sound very possible and it was with highest anticipation that Kate climbed aboard the bus when it swept odoriferously up to their corner.

At the place where the puppies were for sale, a woman met them at the front door and took them around to the back garden where on the lawn in the full sunlight was a wicker basket and in the basket were six little seal brown and white bodies, not one of them much larger than Vic Corsatti's white rat.

At sight of that basket with the six sleepy little pups huddled at the bottom of it, Kate just threw herself on her knees beside it, took the basket up in her arms, and hugged the whole thing to her heart exactly as if she didn't have a lick of sense. Then she set the basket gently down and picked up each baby Boston, fondling it tenderly. One of these was going to be hers. That is, if the price was right.

"The mother of this litter died and these puppies are really too young to sell, but we have to get rid of them, so you can have your pick for five dollars."

Kate looked up at Mr. Tuttle. "You decide," he said.

It was hard. Each one of them was lovable in its own special way. But one seemed to possess more personality than the others. It might have been the way he was marked, for one side of his handsome little head was white, and the other seal brown, and the white side had a dark ear, and the dark side a white one. He was in every way a most distinguished-looking puppy and when he rose shakily in the basket and

barked his irritation at one of his brothers in an infant but meaningful bark, Kate decided that he was in every respect ocean-going.

"I want this one," she said, holding him up, his four legs dangling from the palm of her hand. "This is Skipper."

Mr. Tuttle handed the woman a five-dollar bill, carefully slipped Skipper into his coat pocket, and they caught the next bus home.

"What do you think Mrs. Tuttle will say?" Kate asked as they neared the house.

"My imagination fails me," said Mr. Tuttle. "We will have to use every wile at our command. I am counting on you, Kate."

"I'm counting on Skipper," said Kate, laying her hand lovingly on the warm bulge of Mr. Tuttle's coat pocket.

When they got inside the house, they found Mrs. Tuttle in the living-room reading the Sunday paper. Mr. Tuttle, without a word of warning, walked over to her, slipped Skipper out of his pocket, and laid him in her lap.

"Here's your baby, Martha. You've always wanted one," he said.

Kate watched Mrs. Tuttle in breathless suspense. Everything depended on what she would do in the seconds that followed. In that moment, Skipper's whole future was at stake.

For perhaps thirty seconds Mrs. Tuttle didn't lay a hand on the puppy. She just looked at her husband who refused to meet her eyes. Then she reached down, gathered Skipper to her bosom, said, "The poor little motherless thing. Probably warm milk will be good for him," and rising, went with the puppy to her kitchen. Kate followed, wishing she knew how to do cartwheels. It was difficult to walk in a sensible way when you felt as she did. She couldn't remember when she had ever felt so completely unsensible. And what is more, she liked it.

That evening, before the dusk had deepened into night, Kate tucked Skipper into a warmly padded pasteboard carton and with it held firmly under her arm, started for Lighthouse Avenue with the newest member of the growing Tuttle family. Christopher and Nora would want to see him, of course. And before she returned home, she would drop by at the Corsattis'. Kate very sensibly assumed that her friends would enjoy sharing her pleasures. And Skipper was such a dear. No one could resist him.

No one? Kate stopped on the bottom step of the Tuttles' front porch and looked across to the dark old house of Mrs. Withers. An idea was gradually shaping itself in her mind. There was something she wanted to know about Mrs. Withers, something which had grown out of their talk that day at the beach. In all the time since then, she had had no opportunity to begin another conversation with the queer old lady, but now there was Skipper. Kate started across the front yard.

Mrs. Withers' front steps creaked under her feet as she cautiously climbed them. The big front door with its panes of many-colored glass looked funereal and forbidding. Without waiting even a second, lest her courage should waver, Kate turned the knob on the big flat bell fastened to the door and was rewarded by a loud and rolling ring. The echoes had died away into utter silence before she was able to detect any movement within the house. Then she heard a door creaking somewhere inside, followed by the approach of footsteps. In another moment, the front door was opened a few inches and Mrs. Withers' voice said, "Who's there?"

"It's the girl next door. Kate Summers."

"Well, I'm not buying anything today and I'm not joining anything, so you may run along about your business."

"I'm not selling anything. Honest. I just came to see you."

The door opened another few inches to permit Kate a view of about one third of Mrs. Withers' broad body.

"Why?" she asked.

This stumped Kate for a moment then she remembered Skipper and brought the box forward.

"I have a new puppy and I thought you'd like to see it."

"You could have saved yourself the trouble," returned Mrs. Withers, not even looking into the box. "I don't like dogs. Only cats. And you'd better keep him away from my cat. He doesn't like dogs, either."

"Mrs. Withers," said Kate. She interrupted herself long enough to put the box down between her feet. Straightening up, she looked the old lady steadily in the eye. "Mrs. Withers, do you like anything besides cats?"

"Are you asking to be smart or because you really want to know?"

"Because I really want to know. I've been wondering for a long time."

Mrs. Withers looked out over Kate's head for fully a minute before replying. Then she said slowly, "Yes, I like parrots."

"But not any kind of people?" Kate asked.

Mrs. Withers just looked at her.

"Don't you care whether people like you or not?" persisted Kate. All her life she had considered this of supreme importance because everything depended on it. Food, clothing, friends, everything. It was the reason she had cultivated good sense. It was all she had ever had to give to people and you had to give something in order to receive, otherwise people wouldn't like you. That just stood to reason.

"Don't you care?" she repeated.

"I've never worried much about it," said Mrs. Withers. "I've gone about minding my own business and letting other people mind theirs. That's about all there is to it."

"I guess," said Kate, covering her amazement by stooping to pick up the box with Skipper in it, "I guess you've never needed anybody in your life."

"No, I can't say that I ever have."

"And I guess," continued Kate, moving toward the steps, "nobody has ever needed you."

"If they have, they've never let me know about it."

Kate nodded, her arms tightening around the box while a new conviction grew in her mind.

"You have to need people before you can like them," she said, "and to like you, they have to need you."

Hadn't Nora and Christopher needed her good sense? And hadn't the Tuttles and Cousin Ethel and all the rest of them needed her help? And hadn't they all seemed to like her?

"I've always thought it was the other way around," said Mrs. Withers and closed the door.

Kate went quietly down the steps.

"She's wrong, dead wrong," she said to Skipper. "And she isn't wise, even if she does sound wise sometimes. Christopher said you had to keep your eyes and your mind and your heart open. She's only looked at things with her eyes and mind. She isn't an ocean-going person like you, Skipper. I guess it's true what Cousin Ethel used to say: 'It takes all kinds to make a world.'"

And in her eagerness to escape the atmosphere of the dark old house and to reach the friendliness of Lighthouse Avenue as quickly as possible, Kate never noticed that even shiftless people like Cousin Ethel can at times speak sensibly.

Chapter X

"The Albacore Are Running"

WHILE Kate considered the problem of adoption, the portrait was finished, summer vacation nearly over, and Kate herself had become official cookie baker in the Tuttle house. Still she couldn't make up her mind. If she could be sure that Nora and Christopher would stay put on Lighthouse Avenue or its vicinity, she would have welcomed the Tuttles as parents. But the conviction grew within her that if the Clines should ever leave this town, she, too, wanted to be done with it. Not even Vic's friendship, not Mrs. Tuttle's perfect neatness, nor Mr. Tuttle's shy fondness for her could possibly compensate for their loss. She wouldn't want to stay around to be reminded of her happiness with them; and to have to see the ramshackle little house and its shaggy garden full of surprises, and to know that strangers lived there or, worse, no one at all, was more even than Kate's good sense could bear to face.

Finally after many restless nights when Skipper, curled comfortably on his little mattress alongside Kate's bed, must have wondered at his mistress' twistings and turnings, Kate decided to put the matter squarely to Nora.

So one windy morning, Kate took her problem along with

a box of cookies to Lighthouse Avenue. She was reminded on the way of that time, now so long ago, when she had gone to Nora with the problem of Beverly Jean's birthday party. She hadn't seen anything of Beverly Jean since school closed. It seemed she went away each summer to study dramatics and tap dancing.

"Doesn't she ever have any fun?" Kate had asked when Vic had informed her of the fact.

"I guess the only fun she ever has is when she looks in a mirror," he had answered.

Kate thought of that now. She thought of the portrait, of Skipper, of baking cookies, of the fun she and Vic had had this summer fishing off the wharf, of the times Leo had taken them out for a quick ride in the boat, of the times they had all gone bathing together, the Clines and the Corsattis and herself. And all at once, she felt a little sorry for Beverly Jean. Perhaps you had to pay a price for beauty, too. Just now, it seemed to her that the price was rather high. Perhaps one could be just as happy by being wise without being beautiful. And then Kate took another long step on the road to wisdom. Perhaps, after all, she thought, being cute or pretty wasn't as important as other things, like the things, for instance, that she had been doing all summer.

Nora met her at the door. "Saw you coming," she said. "I was going uptown to shop, but I don't think I want to fight this wind."

"You can almost lean back on it," said Kate, entering on a gust that rattled pictures on the wall near the door.

She handed over the cookies, and while Nora took them

out to the kitchen, planned how best to launch the subject that had brought her here. As usual, she decided that coming right out with it would be the easiest way and the best.

So when Nora returned to Kate and asked, "What's new?" Kate cleared her throat and said, "The Tuttles want to adopt me."

Kate wasn't prepared for the effect of her words.

Nora just looked at Kate while every bit of color drained out of her face and then she said in a small voice, "They do?"

Kate nodded, wondering if Nora were going to faint. She didn't look like Nora at all and Kate began to get scared.

Then Nora turned her back on Kate and went over to the window, "Oh, I wish Christopher were here!"

"Is there anything I can do?" asked Kate, getting up. "Could I go and find him?"

"No," said Nora, coming back to the sofa where Kate had been sitting. "No, let's sit down and talk about it."

"We can talk about it later," said Kate, still worried over Nora's pallor. "You don't look as if you felt very well."

"I'm all right," she said. "What have you decided to do?"

"I haven't decided yet," said Kate, "that's what I came to see you about."

"You mean you want me to help you decide?" cried Nora in something close to a wail.

"Well, not exactly," Kate replied, cautiously. Why on earth was Nora so upset? She wished she had never mentioned the matter.

"Kate, it isn't like you to mince matters," said Nora with some irritation. "Just what *is* on your mind?"

"Well," said Kate, taking the plunge but keeping an apprehensive eye on Nora, "what I wanted to know was whether or not you and Christopher intended to stay in this town for the next ten years?"

Nora swallowed, her eyes, wide and dark, looking fixedly into Kate's, "Why?" she asked.

"Because if you did intend to, I'd let the Tuttles adopt me. You see," Kate went on, "by the end of ten years, I'd be twenty years old and then if you went away, I'd be big enough to go wherever you went and work there."

"You mean," the dark eyes were searching the gray ones now, "you mean you wouldn't want to stay in this place unless Christopher and I were here?"

Kate nodded. "That's right," she said.

Then, as might be expected, Nora did the unexpected. With a cry of, "Oh, my dear," she grabbed Kate to her and began rocking back and forth with her, her arms tightening until Kate almost had the breath squeezed out of her. And all the time Nora kept saying, "Oh, my dear." There wasn't a bit of sense in the performance anywhere, but Kate thought it was about the pleasantest thing that had ever happened to her.

When at last Nora let her go and Kate could look at her again, she saw tear stains on her cheeks, but Kate didn't think they were foolish. They were mixed up somehow with Nora's holding her and calling her "my dear" and not even a sensible person would call tears foolish under such circumstances.

"When do you have to decide?" asked Nora.

"Miss Watson said I could take my time."

"Then," said Nora, "suppose you wait until I have a talk with Christopher and find out about our staying here. It may take him quite a little while to make up his mind, because it naturally would if the next ten years of your life were to depend on it. So you just sit tight and don't say a word to anybody, until I have a talk with you. Agreed?"

"Yes," Kate answered. "It can be another secret."

"That's right," said Nora quickly. "That will be our second secret together and I know already how well I can trust you to keep it, Kate."

When Kate was satisfied that Nora was again her calm and cheerful self, she took leave of her and started for the wharf. It was almost time for the fishing boats to be in. She knew Vic would be there awaiting Leo and everywhere would be bustle and excitement with good-fellowship permeating it all. Kate never missed watching the little boats come home if she could possibly help it. Nearly always, Mrs. Tuttle made it possible.

If the wind had seemed strong before, it was as nothing compared to the gale that whipped around Kate as she progressed along the wharf. The bay was flecked with whitecaps and the gulls seemed blown about like feathered bundles, their melancholy cries swallowed up in the shriek of the wind as it swept between boat houses and tore the tops off breakers. There wasn't the sign of a cloud anywhere, sea and sky were as clean a blue as one could wish. But the waves were huge and the swells that rolled almost under Kate's feet slapped the heavy wharf piling with sullen force.

She found Vic, and together they stood braced against the wind and gazed seaward. So high were the swells and so deep the troughs between them, that they didn't see the fishing fleet until it was well inside the harbor. Eagerly they watched its approach and when the *Lena* hove into sight, "There's Leo," they both cried at once, and Vic started to jig with impatience.

Sturdily the little boats chugged toward the wharf. Kate thought they traveled as far up and down swells as the actual distance they had to cover to gain the wharf. But at last they were maneuvered alongside, and the baskets into which their catches were to be unloaded were lowered to them.

"What luck?" Vic yelled down to Leo from the wharf's edge.

"Albacore," Leo yelled back and winked significantly.

Back to Kate Vic darted with the news.

"Is that good?" she asked, never having heard of albacore before.

"Good?" cried Vic. "It's just about the best. A few boat-loads and you're rich. Well, almost rich," he amended, seeing the amazed, and doubting, expression on Kate's face. "Leo's got a big catch, too," he added.

But when, with the catch unloaded, the fishermen climbed up to the wharf, none of Vic's jubilation was reflected on their faces.

"What's the matter, Louie?" Vic asked, as the old man came toward them. "Didn't you get a boat load?"

Louie paused and turning, shook a fist at the water. "Always it happens," he said bitterly. "All day, every day, you can fish for cod and salmon and sole and smelts and all the rest of it. But on the one day of the season when you run into albacore, there has to be a wind and a sea and a man has the choice of giving up or drowning to get it. And then what good will albacore do him, eh?"

"Is the wind worse out there?" asked Vic.

"Worse?" snorted old Louie with a look of heavy scorn at the heavens. "This is a breeze."

He turned away and Vic and Kate moved over to the edge of the planking to find out what was detaining Leo. He was in the boat, coiling ropes and getting things shipshape again. All his catch had been unloaded.

"Will you take us out for a little bit, Leo?" yelled Vic. "Kate's never been out in a wind."

Leo looked up, frowning with the strain of listening and, as Vic's question reached his ears, he shook his head. "No time," he called back. "I'm going to take on some gasoline and put out again. The albacore are running and boy this is one day I make a killing."

"Let me go with you," cried Vic.

But Leo shook his head. "Too rough," he said. "No place for kids."

"And no place for men," yelled old Louie who had now returned to where Vic and Kate were standing. "You are crazy, Leo."

Other fishermen joined them and echoed what Louie had said. "Don't go, Leo," they pleaded, and something in their earnestness made Vic suddenly apprehensive. Darting away from the little group at the wharf's edge, he ran down the

steps to the float where the *Lena* bobbed and swung. Kate
could see he was pleading with Leo and she was sure he was
not begging to be taken with him. She saw Leo shrug and
grin, heard snatches of their conversation that seemed to in-
dicate that Leo was entirely indifferent both to the urgings
of his fellow fishermen as well as to Vic's.

She saw him smack the gunwale of his boat and nod to Vic
as if he were attempting to reassure him as to the *Lena's*
ocean-going abilities. She wished the wind would stop howl-
ing so that she could hear all of what was said. Then Louie
and three other men joined Vic on the float. But still Leo
shrugged and laughed and made ready to put out again. She
could see it was useless to dissuade him from his intention.
He would make that killing in spite of all that was being said
against it. Could it be as dangerous as they said? Wasn't Leo
the best fisherman on the bay? Hadn't he told her once that
he and the *Lena* had weathered many storms, that she was
his girl friend and had never let him down? But then, hadn't
he told her on that same day that he didn't have good sense?
Was he being sensible now?

While these things were going through Kate's mind, Leo
cast off, the chug of the *Lena's* motor almost silenced by the
gale. Once he looked up, saw her standing there, and waved.
She waved back and a little of her previous confidence in
Leo returned. A grown man wouldn't bother to wave to a
little girl if he were going into danger. He'd be too much worried about the danger to bother. But that's where Kate was
wrong. Brave men don't worry about danger and heroes are
apt to have more courage than good sense. If Leo was no

hero, at least he was brave, and if he lacked good sense, he never lacked courage. What he did, he did because he believed he had to do it, because he considered it the sensible thing to do. To him, the game was worth the risk. Let others play it safely if they wished. But the albacore were running and he had to make a killing. What matter wind and sea? *The albacore were running.*

Slowly the group on the float climbed back to the wharf and Vic rejoined Kate.

"He shouldn't have gone," said Vic, his eyes still following the churning *Lena* which looked smaller and more helpless with every passing minute. It was the only boat out there, and Kate thought that this fact alone made the ocean suddenly seem larger and rougher than it had before. But she didn't say so to Vic. Instead she said, "You told me yourself once that Leo was the best fisherman on the bay. It stands to reason he can go where the others can't."

"The others said he wouldn't come back," replied Vic with a catch in his voice that made Kate turn quickly to him. Was Vic really that scared? His eyes were suspiciously moist, but that might be the work of the wind.

"When did Leo say he'd be back?" she asked, as casually as possible.

"He said he might be out all night waiting for the storm to blow over."

Several times that night, Kate awoke to wonder whether Leo had safely returned with his killing or whether he were tossing helplessly on the dark and windy sea. She thought of

Vic and knew that he would be gazing into the dark, too, and thinking the same thoughts. She wished it were possible for him to know that she was awake and worrying with him. As his girl friend, it was her responsibility to stand by him in this crisis, to make his troubles her own, and to help him if she could. It might have been some comfort for him to have known how she felt about it. Once, she got out of bed and went to the dresser from which she took the red bandanna handkerchief Leo had given her the first day she had ever met him. She put it under her pillow and crept back into bed. It was silly, of course, but it made Leo seem closer and safer to have his gift where she could touch it.

But the next morning brought no gallant little *Lena* chugging up to the wharf. Instead, a sober group of fishermen stood looking vaguely out at the now quiet water and sorrowfully shaking their heads.

"But he has been out as long as this before," Christopher who had shown as much concern as anyone, argued in an effort to be reassuring.

But the men who toiled on the water refused to be convinced. "No small boat could live in such a sea," they insisted, and as the day advanced and still Leo failed to return it seemed more and more certain that they were right.

Only Vic held to the hope that Leo would come safely home. "He's better than all those other guys. He could get through where they couldn't. Maybe it was too rough to fish when he got out there yesterday and so he rode it out and stayed to fish today."

"Well, the boats are putting out again this morning, and when they come back, we'll know the answer," said Christopher.

With stubborn hope, they watched the boats depart once more for the fishing grounds. Would Leo be with them when they returned home again? Only the sea, sparkling and shimmering this morning as if repentant over yesterday's ugly mood, could give the answer.

But when toward evening the fleet drew up to the wharf, no Leo came with it. Eagerly, tensely, Kate and Vic and Christopher, along with a large group of townspeople, strained their eyes for sight of the *Lena*. But this time Leo's "girl friend" had let him down.

"Not even a piece of wreckage," Kate heard one of the men tell Christopher. She turned to Vic, but after one glance at his stricken face, she quickly looked away. It was terrible when a person was struggling to withhold tears. It was worse than if he cried. Why didn't he cry? No one would think less of him. They all knew how he worshiped Leo. Why, she believed, it was even sensible sometimes to cry. Like now. She was having a terribly hard time to keep from crying herself, but if Vic didn't, she wouldn't.

All that day, Vic remained at the wharf. Not Christopher, not Kate, not all his family could persuade him to leave.

"He probably thinks that as long as he is still waiting, it isn't all over, that Leo might still come home. That's what he thinks," Kate said very low to Christopher when, in the afternoon, they came again to remonstrate with him. "The minute he really turns his back on the ocean and leaves the wharf, then that's the end. He's given Leo up for good then."

Christopher looked at her with interest. "How do you know that?" he asked.

"I just know," replied Kate.

"And do you consider that sensible?" asked Christopher.

"Yes, if it makes Vic feel any better," returned Kate.

"You may be right," said Christopher, after a brief silence. "Let's go home and leave him here with his hope, his courage, and his grief."

Many hours later, Kate opened her eyes to the darkness of her bedroom. She didn't know what had awakened her, but it was as if someone had called. She listened, but heard no sound except Skipper's quiet breathing from the floor beside the bed. She got to her knees and looked out of the window. Down at the corner, the street light was burning and a light shown in the house across the way. It couldn't be awfully late, she decided. She crouched there for a full minute conscious of the sound of breakers, noticing that tonight they were no louder than usual. She wondered if from now on she would always listen to them with special interest. Until a few hours ago, it had never mattered in the least whether they were noisy or quiet. But lately she had learned how much depended on that difference.

Had Leo come home yet? Would Vic run over to tell her if he had? Was he perhaps outside, now, waiting for her to come down? Perhaps he was the one who had wakened her. He would hesitate, she knew, to rouse the whole house.

She stuck her head out of the window. "Vic," she called softly. "Vic."

There was no answer. For another moment she sat there, then resolutely she got off the bed and began to put on her clothes. She drew a sweater over her dress and slipped Skipper's harness on him. In front of the dresser, she paused a moment and took something out of the top drawer, then, with the dog in her arms, she descended the stairs to the front hall. As she opened the front door, it creaked ever so little, and she waited breathlessly, holding Skipper as still as possible. But no one came out of Mrs. Tuttle's room, so Kate slipped through the door and onto the dark porch.

As she set Skipper down, she knew that if she were caught, going forth into the night alone and without permission, the matter of her adoption would be settled. The Tuttles would want nothing further to do with her. They had always been able to rely on her doing what was expected of her, and here she was sallying forth into the night in a most unreliable if not downright disobedient and wicked manner. And she was doing it on a mere hunch. Nothing more. But Kate knew as surely as she knew she was walking toward the beach, that whatever might happen to her as a result of this night's wandering, she could not have remained a minute longer in the house. She had somehow got the conviction sitting there in the window that Vic needed her, and she thought she knew where she could find him. The wharf was closed to all traffic after eight o'clock, but that wouldn't prevent Vic's waiting somewhere along the beach.

It was dark on the sand. There were no street lights here and Kate looked for comfort to the hills back of the town

where houselights twinkled friendly eyes at her, as bright as
the stars just above them. Trudging forward on the yielding
sand, Kate thought the lights looked like stars that had slid
downhill, then smiled at the idea, which was pretty silly. As
if stars could slide downhill!

All at once, Skipper stopped so quickly Kate bumped into
him. He growled and pressed for protection against her legs.
Skipper was fully aware at the moment that he was not yet a
grown dog.

Kate strained her eyes into the darkness and at last made
out an object a little darker than the sand on which it was
sitting. She drew near it slowly, shoving the cringing Skipper
ahead of her.

"Vic," she said.

There was a quick sniff, a quicker motion of a hand. "That
you, Kate?" said a muffled voice.

"Yes, it's me," and Kate slid to her knees on the sand beside him.

"Whatcha doing out here?"

"I couldn't sleep," said Kate.

"Did they say you could come?"

"No."

"You'll catch it when they find out," Vic said, sniffing
again.

"Here," said Kate. "I remember you said you never bothered to carry one."

Vic reached out and in the dark Kate put a folded handkerchief into his hand. It was a red bandanna.

163

"It's big," said Vic, shaking it out.

"Yes," said Kate. "Leo gave it to me the first day he took us out in the *Lena* together. I thought you'd like to have it back."

For a moment the two sat motionless on the cold sand while the breakers smashed and receded hissingly along the beach. Then, quietly, Vic began to cry into the red bandanna.

Kate did nothing and said nothing. She just sat and let him cry. She was deciding that there are times when all the good sense in the world is of no avail and of no purpose. It was a disagreeable decision because she would have felt better doing something, saying something that would help Vic. Just to sit there like a lump, made her unhappier than ever. But had Kate been a little wiser, she would have known that it takes good sense to arrive at that decision.

After a while Vic said, "You ought to get home before somebody finds out you're gone."

"I won't go till you do," Kate answered.

"What'll happen if they catch you?"

"They'll probably send me back to Miss Watson and the county office."

Vic got up immediately. "Come on," he said and pulled Kate to her feet.

Together they started up the beach in the direction of home. At the Tuttles' front door they halted.

"Thanks for the handkerchief," said Vic.

"It's O.K.," Kate answered, and gathering Skipper under one arm, went inside.

164

After closing the front door and with Skipper still dangling helplessly, she paused to watch Vic cross the corner diagonally under the street light on his way to Lighthouse Avenue.

Then, very quietly, Kate climbed the stairs to bed.

Chapter XI

Needed for Good

IT WAS a month after that night on the beach that Kate was again wakened out of sound sleep. Only this time someone actually was there to do the waking. Mrs. Tuttle was bending over her when she opened her eyes and was saying, "Wake up, Kate. It's Christopher. He's downstairs and wants to see you about some secret."

For an instant, Kate lay there marshaling her wits. Christopher. Secret. All at once it dawned on her. *The secret.* Mrs. Tuttle had to dodge the bedclothes as Kate flung them to one side and began fumbling for her slippers.

"Did he say . . . Do you know?" demanded Kate, digging frantically for an arm of her dressing gown.

"No, I don't know a thing," declared Mrs. Tuttle, but she was smiling so happily that Kate felt pretty sure she knew something.

Down the stairs went Kate, not quietly this time, but racing recklessly with Skipper falling over her heels. In the front hall stood a beaming Christopher and a sleepy Mr. Tuttle.

"Nora just sent me to tell you first of all that the secret has arrived. That's what she told me to say."

Kate was so excited that her teeth were chattering, but she managed to say, "Is it . . . ?"

"It's a boy," answered Christopher, beaming more than ever. "His name is Jim Cline. I think you'll like him."

"When can I see him?"

"Tomorrow. But you'll have to view him through a glass wall, I believe."

"And Nora's all right?"

"Nora's fine. She'll be home in a week."

"We'll have to get the house cleaned before then," said Kate more to herself than to Christopher.

The grown-ups laughed. "Two o'clock in the morning, a new citizen not over three hours old to talk about, and you have to bring up house cleaning. It's refreshingly like you, Kate," said Christopher.

"This is Tuesday," Kate went on, thinking out loud. "I could do it Sunday and probably she'll be home Monday. Even if she came Tuesday, it wouldn't be very bad if Christopher was careful. And I could drop in Monday evening to straighten it up."

"We can plan all that at dinner tomorrow," said Mrs. Tuttle. "Christopher, we'd like you to have it with us. Sort of a celebration. A Jim Cline doesn't come into this world every day of the week."

"That's just what I was thinking," said Mr. Tuttle and disappeared into the hall closet.

"What on earth—?" began his wife, as they heard him rummaging around inside.

When he emerged at last, he had a package in his hand.

"It's sherry," he explained. "Rather good, I believe. I've been saving it for a really important occasion like this one. We'll toast young Jim and then Christopher can get off to bed. You look as if you could do with some sleep."

"Andrew Tuttle!" exclaimed Mrs. Tuttle. "How long has that been in my hall closet?"

"It's been in our hall closet about a year and a half. Had it hidden in a rubber boot," answered Mr. Tuttle, imperturbably. "Come on into the kitchen everybody. Yes, you too, Kate. A sip won't hurt you any, and young Jim will be better off for your good wishes."

So, around the kitchen table, they toasted young Jim.

"How on earth did you happen to name him that?" asked Mrs. Tuttle.

"Wanted something as different from 'Christopher' as I could get," explained the young gentleman's father.

"He'll never be an artist with that name," declared Mr. Tuttle, quirking up one corner of his mustache. There was a twinkle in his eye.

"Sounds more like a politician to me," said Mrs. Tuttle.

Kate's eyes, as deep as wells and full of wonder and speculation, were lifted now to Christopher. "Do politicians ever get to be president?" she asked.

Christopher studied the amber liquid in his glass for an instant. "I believe it has occurred now and then," he said.

"Because," she added, firmly, "Jim is going to be president. Nora and I decided that a long time ago."

"Then that settles it," declared Christopher, setting down his glass. "Thank you, for everything," he said, looking toward the Tuttles. "Shall I pick you up after school, Kate?"

"Yes," she replied, then added with a sigh, "I don't think I'll be much good at school tomorrow."

"You won't if you don't get some more sleep," affirmed Mrs. Tuttle.

So they said good-night to Christopher who left with all kinds of good wishes for Nora and young Jim ringing in his ears. Kate lay for a while thinking about the future. It would be wonderful having a baby to care for again. She had missed babies at the Tuttle house. Nora had promised that she could help take care of hers. Kate had tended many, and had loved them all. But she was prepared to believe that Jim Cline would be the very nicest of the whole lot.

So far, Nora had not mentioned to her the possibility of their staying here for the next ten years. Doubtless, Christopher hadn't made up his mind about it yet. Should she take a chance on it and let the Tuttles adopt her? Or should she wait for Christopher's decision. As she drifted off to sleep Kate felt a little twinge of envy for young Jim Cline. But it was entirely different from the envy she had once felt for Beverly Jean. It was just good sense to envy anyone who happened to have Nora and Christopher for parents. Even if he was only three hours old. Four hours, now, she corrected herself, and fell asleep.

When Nora and Jim came home a week later in the company of Christopher and a woman in formidably starched white who turned out to be a nurse named Mrs. Swanson, she found a clean house and Kate awaiting them.

"I don't see why Jim couldn't have been born during vacation," said Kate, who sat in the largest chair with the small-est Cline held adoringly in her arms.

"And the doctor couldn't understand why he didn't come in the daytime instead of in the middle of the night," added Christopher. "Jim seems to have started off by not pleasing anybody."

"Don't forget," called Nora from the bedroom, "that he obliged pretty thoroughly by just being Jim."

"He's terribly homely," said Kate, watching Jim's minute fingers curling around her thumb.

"Well, how do you like that!" exclaimed Christopher, in-dignantly. "A nice way to talk about my first-born son. Here, give me that baby."

He took a step toward Kate, but she just rolled the tiny bundle closer to her heart and grinned across it at him.

"It's a good sign," she exclaimed. "Cousin Ethel always said that the homeliest babies make the prettiest grown-ups."

"Do they?" demanded Christopher.

"I don't know," answered Kate soberly. "I didn't stay to see any of hers grow up, but they were certainy homely ba-bies. Not as homely as Jim, though," she added happily.

"That's a relief," said Christopher. "And now before your compliments turn Jim's head, I think you'd better hand him over to Mrs. Swanson. It's his feeding time."

As Kate followed the nurse into the bedroom, she didn't see a messenger boy come up to the front door. But Christo-pher saw him and was at the door before he had a chance to ring the bell. He handed Christopher a telegram which he signed for and read standing in the doorway. Two or three

times he read the message, then without a word to anyone, he walked straight out of the house and over to the Tuttles. Since it was a Sunday morning, he would find them both at home.

What took place after he got there was known to Kate and Nora when he returned to his own house an hour later. Just one hour, but in that space of time, Kate's problem was solved and though it seemed queer in the light of her previous concern about the matter, it would no longer worry her in the least whether the Clines remained on Lighthouse Avenue or journeyed to darkest Africa. Because, wherever they journeyed, Kate would go along, too.

Christopher found her in the kitchen with Mrs. Swanson.

"Come into the bedroom, Kate," he said to her. "Nora and I want to talk with you."

Kate looked up at him in alarm. Christopher had never spoken in that tone to her before. His face was white and all the freckles stood out plainly on it. She hadn't realized that Christopher had so many. But what was the trouble? It must be trouble, he sounded so serious. Had she done something wrong? Lately she had so often done what wasn't expected of her that it was hard to know whether she should feel scared or not. Life had certainly been simpler when she had always acted sensibly. But she had to admit as she followed slowly after the tall man striding before her, that it was certainly a lot more fun now than it used to be.

Nora's smile was reassuring as she entered the room and Christopher shut the door. But she could easily imagine Nora smiling at anyone who was in trouble just to make them feel better. She wasn't at all sure at the moment whether it was a sensible thing to do or not.

"Sit down," ordered Christopher, still in that solemn way. Kate sat.

" 'Sensible Kate' has won the contest," said Christopher.

Kate smiled and her eyes, warm with love and faith, sought his. "That proves you're a good artist, doesn't it?" she cried.

"I don't know what it proves, Kate. I don't know that it proves anything, but it makes something possible that wasn't possible before. In a manner of speaking, I am now a successful artist whether or not I am a very good one. As you would put it, Kate, I'll now be able to make a living. So good a one, in fact, that I shall be able easily to support four people."

He looked at Kate with a little of his old teasing expression in his eyes. Kate's face was blandly matter-of-fact.

"Is Mrs. Swanson going to stay for good?" she asked.

Nora threw her head back against the pillow in a hearty laugh. "You might as well save your climaxes, Christopher, they're wasted on Kate."

"No," said Christopher, "she isn't, but we thought, Nora and I, that perhaps you would."

Now, suddenly, it was all as plain as day to Kate. Why hadn't she thought of it before? Christopher and Nora would need a family helper now. Naturally Nora couldn't keep house and take care of Jim, too. And it wouldn't hurt the Tuttles' feelings, either, because they'd understand that Nora needed her more. They were understanding people. And even after she was too old to be on the county, or rather, *of* the county, she'd still stay and work for Christopher and Nora. She'd work for them all the rest of her life if she could just be with them. It was a perfect solution of the problem. Why, it hadn't really been a problem at all. She hadn't used her head, that was all.

This was going through Kate's head at the same time that she was assuring Christopher and Nora that she'd stay.

"You need me more than the Tuttles. I'm sure they'll let me leave. We can see Miss Watson tomorrow and fix it up. They'll even pay you something, you know, for taking care of me."

Kate was surprised to see a strange look come over Nora's face and to hear Christopher say in shocked tones, "What on earth are you talking about?"

Kate thought it was up to Christopher to say what he meant since she had made her own position perfectly plain. Why didn't he understand her? Had she jumped to conclusions? She remembered with some alarm that other time when she had done so, thinking she was being taken away. But Christopher had said he hoped she would stay for good. For good. There was something in those two words that seemed to suggest a condition which was settled and certain. They seemed to eliminate Miss Watson and the county. For good seemed an awfully long time, longer even than growing up. So Kate sat without saying a word, waiting for the grown-ups to explain themselves.

She didn't have to wait very long. Christopher reached across the few inches of space that separated their chairs and drew her to his knees.

"It's like this, Kate," he began. "Nora and I have been thinking for some time that we really needed someone with

175

good sense around permanently. It didn't seem fair to Jim to let him grow up at the mercy of two parents who didn't possess a lick of it. We decided that next to having a father or a mother who were sensible, having a sister who was, would be about the finest thing that could happen to a fellow like Jim. Besides, I don't want to risk losing such a model as you. So we are asking you right now, this very minute, if you would very much mind being Jim's sister for the rest of your natural life."

Kate turned in his arms to look at him. "You want to adopt me?" she asked.

"Yes," answered Christopher.

"We've known we wanted to for quite a while," said Nora while Kate sat with bowed head trying to act sensibly instead of like a baby. There was certainly nothing to cry about at the prospect of living forever with Nora and Christopher. "But we couldn't ask you until Christopher was sure he was in a position to ask," Nora continued. "It was one thing for Jim to live our hand and mouth existence. He couldn't have helped himself, poor dear, but we had no right to ask you to share it with us. But now we can ask you and so we do," she finished. "On account of 'Sensible Kate.' You see, you've had a pretty big finger in your own pie, haven't you?"

Then Kate said a surprising thing, not at all the sort of thing you would expect her to say. She didn't even mention adoption; she didn't even answer Christopher's question. Instead, she said, "I guess being sensible is better than being pretty or cute, after all. And it's not the picture winning the contest that makes me think so, either. It's because you two want me because I'm sensible. You need me on account of it. You need me for good."

Christopher gave her a tremendous hug. "Then you'll let us adopt you?" he asked.

"Oh, yes," said Kate. "That's what I've wanted right along. That is, I've wanted to be near you. But what will the Tuttles say?"

"They've already said," declared Christopher. "Mr. Tuttle told me he thought you'd like to have a pair of grandparents to visit now and then, like any other little girl. And Mrs. Tuttle said she would depend on you for cookies. And, of course, Skipper goes where you go. So that settles that."

Chapter XII

"Sensible Kate"

KATE was standing up in front of the whole class making an announcement. It was just like being the teacher, making an announcement all by herself. Everyone was listening carefully because Kate was inviting the sixth grade, each one of them and no one especially, to her birthday party on the following Saturday. It was to be a candy pull and no one was to bring presents, but everyone was to bring an apron. Even the boys.

It would be Kate's first birthday party and the last one she would ever give in the little house on Lighthouse Avenue. For Christopher was moving his family, which now of course included Kate, to another house, larger and with a view of the sea. Kate would again have a room of her own. Just now, she was sharing one with Jim Cline, but she didn't mind a bit. No sensible person could object to having such an agreeable companion as young Jim around. He slept like a top and if she stayed at her mirror a little longer than was necessary now and then, Jim, though he might watch her with strangely wise eyes, could be depended on never to say a word.

During the last few days, Kate had spent more time than

usual before that mirror. Christopher had sent for and received the portrait that had won the contest. He had asked to borrow it for Kate's birthday. "A private showing," he had said. Kate had been even more pleased than she had let on. Because, there was no use trying to evade the fact, the picture portrayed her in a most attractive way. It would be gratifying to have her classmates see her appearing so.

Now the thing that was worrying Kate was not whether or not it was better to be sensible or pretty. That question she had already answered. What bothered her now was whether or not she was actually as good-looking as that portrait showed her to be. It was unquestionably her face, but also unquestionably there were things added to it. And subtracted. For instance, the freckles. There was merely a suggestion of them in the picture, whereas in reality Kate's face was generously sprinkled. This she had brought to the attention of Christopher when the picture was unwrapped.

"It would have taken too long to put them all in, Kate," he had answered. "After all, there was a deadline on the contest, you know."

"But she looks better without them," Kate had muttered. She always referred to "Sensible Kate" as "she."

"So would you," Nora had added, "but do you think it would be worth wearing a hat for eternally and all the time? I think I'd rather have freckles."

"I would, too," Kate had agreed.

It was a proud moment for Kate, standing up in front of the class. She could see all the eyes turned upon her, Beverly Jean's with the rest. Would Beverly Jean come to her party, she wondered? There was still a coolness between them. Beverly Jean had scrupulously ignored the portrait, although the details of Christopher's success had been thoroughly set forth in the local newspaper. It had even mentioned his model, Kate Summers, "whom Mr. and Mrs. Cline have legally adopted."

Kate had saved the clipping, putting it away in her handkerchief box with a couple of valentines she had there. She didn't greatly care if Beverly Jean came to the party or didn't. Sometimes she even hoped a tiny bit that she wouldn't.

One may be pardoned for wanting the spotlight all to himself on one's eleventh birthday. Especially when it is the first time one has ever held that spot. Still there would be wholesome satisfaction in having Beverly Jean see that portrait and to know, as she would certainly know as she looked at it, that that face, Kate's face, would be multiplied thousands of times and would brighten the newsstands of every city in the country, just like the face of a movie actress. Yes, there would certainly be satisfaction in that.

Mr. and Mrs. Tuttle were coming to the party. Mr. Tuttle would probably come late, after everyone else had gone, but they were staying on for dinner, so they would be part of the private showing and of Kate's more or less formal presentation as the daughter of Christopher and Nora. Mrs. Tuttle was coming early to help Nora with the candy.

Though it was now the middle of November, Kate's birthday outdid itself in the matter of climate. Even the elements seemed determined that this first party should be a success. It would be plenty warm enough to allow the boys and girls to pull their taffy outdoors.

"And a lucky thing for you," commented Mrs. Tuttle to Nora as she tied an apron around her ample figure and prepared to "pitch in." Mrs. Tuttle always managed to make any domestic activity take on the flavor of a major conflict. "All those young ones pulling candy all over your house would have been something, I can tell you."

"Oh, we'd have lived through it, all right," Nora comforted her. "Candy washes out of things easily. Especially taffy."

Mrs. Tuttle reached for the molasses without comment, and Kate left them to inspect the spotless living-room for the one-hundredth time. "Sensible Kate" reposed in state on Christopher's largest easel. Kate wondered how she would be able to keep from looking at it all afternoon. Because, of course, she couldn't pay any attention to it while her guests were there. They would think she was admiring herself! "Well, wasn't she?" a little voice asked way down inside of her. Before she could answer that little voice, Christopher came into the room, young Jim in his arms.

Kate whirled from the picture, but not before Christopher had noted her there. Something in the way he looked at her made Kate blush and the harder she tried not to, the warmer her cheeks got.

"How does it feel to be eleven?" he asked. "I've forgotten, it's been such a long time ago."

"I think I feel just the same as I did yesterday," said Kate. Thank goodness, the warmth was leaving her face.

"I'm very glad to hear that," answered Christopher. "You see, I liked you very much when you were ten. In fact, I liked you better than any little girl I ever knew up to that time. I hope you'll try to stay just the way you were then."

"But I can't," laughed Kate. "I'll keep growing up all the time."

"That's perfectly true," replied Christopher, pulling the end of his tie out of Jim's mouth. "But that needn't prevent your continuing to be sensible, need it?"

"No," said Kate, "I guess not."

"I have a feeling, Kate," said Christopher, sounding very solemn, for him. "I have a feeling that it is now time for me to give you my first piece of fatherly advice."

"Yes?" Kate began to have a good idea of what was coming next.

"Until now," said Christopher, "various people, including Nora and I, have had need of your good sense. But I think from this day forth, the person who is going to have most need of it is a young lady, an artist's model, named Kate Summers."

Kate didn't say anything, and after a little pause, Christopher went on talking.

"It has been demonstrated many times, my dear, that fame has the power to turn the head of even sensible people. In a very small way, you have acquired fame. Your good sense brought it to you. I sincerely hope that now your good sense will protect you from its possible pitfalls. I'd hate to think I had a daughter that was getting sort of full of herself."

Vic's arrival broke up the conversation before Kate had a chance to reply. But Christopher's words had struck home and had shown her how close she had been to becoming a counterpart of Beverly Jean. Being sensible was still more important than anything else. She must never forget that fact.

Even though they had gone into a new room at school, Kate still considered herself Vic's girl friend. So far, Vic had given no intimations that the relationship might be at an end. In spite of the fact that Leo had died without ever having made that "killing" he so ardently longed for, he had provided well for his young brother. An insurance policy which named Vic as beneficiary and which would be payable at the end of seven years when the law would declare Leo officially dead, was to bring to Vic two thousand dollars.

"Enough for me to buy a boat. A better boat than Leo's," Vic had told Kate when he had confided the news. "I'm eleven now and in seven years I'll be eighteen. Just right for buying a boat and going to sea. I'm going to name it *Leo's Lena.*"

"Oh, Vic," Kate had exclaimed. "That's a perfect name."

"And if you're still my girl friend I'll take you out in it," he had added.

"I probably won't be around here then," Kate had replied somewhat loftily. After all, Vic needn't think she was just going to hang around anxiously waiting for a ride in his boat.

"Where'll you be?" he had asked quickly.

"Christopher and Nora want me to go to college, so, of course, I'm going. I'm going to be a home-making teacher."

"You don't have to be taught how to do that. Girls are just supposed to know," Vic had scoffed.

"Well, Nora sure didn't," Kate had replied. "And she said I'd be a genius at teaching it because I had done such a thorough job on her. She said I'd even managed to give her an inferiority complex about it."

"What's that?" Vic had demanded.

"I don't know," Kate had confessed, "but it must be something good if Nora has it."

Hardly had Vic been welcomed, when the others began to arrive and soon the little house was bulging with children. Jim had been packed off to his bedroom from whence his howls of protest could be heard over the general din and havoc. As soon as everyone was there, everyone, that is, except Beverly Jean, Nora ordered them to put on their aprons and line up at the kitchen door. At first, the boys seemed a little hesitant, but when Christopher hung on himself one of Nora's daintiest concoctions of lawn and lace as far as it would go down the six feet of him, the boys with a shout of laughter at the ridiculous figure he cut, put on theirs and the party really began.

As soon as each guest had been handed his hunk of taffy, he marched outside through the back door and began the job of pulling. A prize was to be given the boy and girl who got their candy the whitest. Since whiteness could only be achieved by hard pulling, the winner would really earn his reward.

Kate was having the time of her life pulling candy as if her life depended on it, when Nora stuck her head out of the kitchen door and called, "Kate, will you come here a minute?"

At the door Nora said, "Another guest is here. Beverly Jean."

"Then she really came," exclaimed Kate, in tones of astonishment.

"Here, hand me that candy and wash your hands at the sink. Mrs. Tuttle is entertaining her in the living-room."

"Wouldn't you know she'd get here after everyone else?" Kate giggled, as she rubbed taffy off her sticky fingers.

"Yes, but it missed fire this time. No one was around to greet her but Mrs. Tuttle and me."

Feeling suddenly a little shy, Kate entered the living-room and greeted Beverly Jean.

"Where is everybody?" asked Beverly Jean.

"Outside pulling taffy," answered Kate, then, realizing all at once that Beverly Jean would soon be doing the same thing, she added, "did you bring an apron?"

"No," said Beverly Jean, in a good imitation of a tired voice. "I decided not to pull candy. It's so terribly messy."

"Nonsense," came Nora's voice from behind the little girls. "It's the most fun you can think of. Come on, Beverly Jean. I'll give you one of Kate's dresses and apron you up to the chin. We'll even tie your curls up so there won't be a thing about you it can hurt."

"Oh, no," Beverly Jean started to protest. But she hadn't reckoned on Nora. And before she knew what was happening she found herself propelled by a firm hand on her shoulder in the direction of the bedroom. There, she was handed one of Kate's least fussy dresses and told to hurry up. "The others have a big start on you," Nora added, just as if she thought that would worry Beverly Jean.

A few minutes later, she emerged and for the first time in her life, Kate realized how far clothes can go in the matter of glamour. Beverly Jean in a faded green gingham seemed divested of that strange indefinable aura that had seemed to stand between her and those lesser mortals who comprised her audience. Then, Nora finished the job. Stepping forward with the remark, "Now you look ready to have a good time," and deaf to Beverly Jean's somewhat frantic protests, Nora proceeded to pin up her curls with bobby pins.

When that was done, Beverly Jean's metamorphosis into a new individual was complete. For perhaps the first time in her life, Beverly Jean looked like a little girl instead of a movie queen. But she didn't look like a very happy little girl. She was angry, as thoroughly angry as she had probably ever been. But somehow it was becoming. Gone was her habitual pout and the querulous look that always lurked in her lovely eyes. Now they blazed and her mouth was set in a firm line of rage at the indignity that had been thrust upon her. It made her chin resolute instead of merely pretty, and her ears which Kate was seeing for the first time were as perfect as all her other features.

"Now," said Nora, happily indifferent to Beverly Jean's wrath, "come into the kitchen and we'll give you your taffy."

A moment later, a hunk of it was thrust into Beverly Jean's reluctant but helpless hand, and she was frankly shoved through the back door into the garden, Kate just behind her.

"Look at Beverly Jean," came a cry from several voices at once, and smiling instinctively at the spotlight, Beverly Jean, with what dignity was left to her, advanced toward the amazed and delighted group.

"Well, I'll be—," Kate heard Christopher mutter, and then, advancing to meet the latecomer, he said, loudly, "Hello, Beverly Jean. You're a welcome sight. The only girl here with sense enough to know how to dress for a candy pull. Kate, and all you others, why didn't you think to put your hair on top of your head? You'll wish you had when it gets gummed up in the taffy."

To Kate's utter astonishment, she saw Beverly Jean bridle and smirk at this allusion to her good sense. Was it possible that she actually considered it more important than good looks? But no, Kate assured herself almost immediately. Beverly Jean was only making the most of a bad moment. And even in that get-up, she could be perfectly certain that she was still the prettiest girl there. But, at least, Christopher's compliment had put out the fires in her eyes. Now Beverly Jean was as charming and affable as it was possible for her to be. Which is saying a good deal.

When the candy had been pulled and the prizes awarded (Beverly Jean had been unable to catch up with the others and so her candy was the darkest of the lot), they all went into the house where Nora gave them waxed paper to wrap their candy in, and sat them on the floor for ice cream and cake. Kate couldn't help being glad that Beverly Jean was still wearing her old dress. She might have objected to the floor otherwise. At one end of the room was the easel bearing "Sensible Kate." It was covered and had been since Vic's arrival. Now Christopher went over to it and everyone stopped eating to watch him.

"Kate," he said, "I herewith present to you your first birthday present as our daughter. You can't actually take possession of it for a while, but as soon as those people back East get through with it, you are to become the owner of 'Sensible Kate.'"

With that, Christopher lifted away the cloth, and for the first time, Kate's classmates beheld this picture of her which was to become familiar before long to thousands of people throughout the country. There was an embarrassed murmur, but not a sound from Kate. It was to be hers! Always and forever, she would be able to look upon this tangible proof of the wisdom of good sense. It would be a constant reminder of the importance of wisdom. It would help her along that far-reaching road. And some day perhaps, if she remained true to the things in that picture, she would become wise. And maybe beautiful. Because this picture was the evidence of what she might become. She knew that now. It was Sensible Kate, not Kate Summers. Something of herself was there, of course, but there was more, much more, that no one could see in her face if they were to look at it now. But Christopher had seen. Because he knew how she felt about things, he had put it all in the portrait as a kind of promise of what might be. No danger now, that she would lose her head over whatever fame this picture might achieve!

"It doesn't look much like her," observed Beverly Jean.

"It does, too," Vic contradicted her hotly.

"You are both right," Christopher's quiet voice silenced the two antagonists. "When an artist does anyone's portrait, he puts into it what is in that person's heart as well as what appears on his face. To those of us who know her and love her, it looks exactly like Kate."

Beverly Jean could add nothing to that, so discreetly kept silent as Kate looked up at Christopher with her heart in her eyes.

When the last of the guests had gone, except of course Mrs. Tuttle, Kate and Nora and Christopher stood together in front of the easel. Mrs. Tuttle was rocking Jim who had already become a cuddled baby.

"I couldn't thank you in front of all of them," Kate said. "I couldn't think of anything to say except 'Thank you' and that wouldn't have sounded important enough."

"It would have to me," said Christopher.

"But I do thank you," said Kate. "I thank you both. And there's something I'd like to say to prove it."

"What's that?" asked Nora, putting an arm around Kate's waist.

"It's just this," replied Kate. "I'd rather be Sensible Kate than anyone else in the world. Even a movie actress."

And she meant it.